Keith has enjoyed a diverse career to date. Graduating from Glasgow University with a Master's degree in Politics, he first went into the world of finance. From there, he moved into defence sales, quickly rising to senior managerial and director positions. At one stage, he commanded a Europe-wide defence sector sales team and would travel daily to one European country after another. This first 'spell' in the defence sector quickly pulled him in for good.

He speedily learned about the secretive side of commercial defence-related products and services and his next move into working as a security-cleared contractor for the Ministry of Defence in Whitehall was an obvious move.

Within this role, Keith would spend much of his time in or around military establishments for all three arms of the Service, working also with high-ranking officers and having his first experience of British Special Forces.

From the MoD, he moved to a classified position (Top Secret) within the British Foreign and Commonwealth Office in London. This secretive role brought him in touch with a huge array of other law enforcement and security intelligence service personnel. Today, he continues to work, periodically, in this environment.

I wish to thank Kathryn, my wife, for her support and her patience. To Lisa, you have been a great help. Two key women in my writing life.

Keith Turnbull

ROGUE WARRIOR

Hey John

Hope you enjoy

[signature]

AUSTIN MACAULEY PUBLISHERS™

LONDON • CAMBRIDGE • NEW YORK • SHARJAH

A CIP catalogue record for this title is available from the British Library.

ISBN 9781528932110 (Paperback)
ISBN 9781528932127 (Kindle e-book)
ISBN 9781528966924 (ePub e-book)

www.austinmacauley.com

First Published (2019)
Austin Macauley Publishers Ltd
25 Canada Square
Canary Wharf
London
E14 5LQ

Shoshanna, you know who you are.

Alexander Prokhorenko, a brave soldier.

Chapter 1
Origin

She had been there for a while, but exactly how long, she didn't know. Just that it had been quite a time. One day seemed to merge methodically and routinely into the next, with each seeming to have the same storyline. Wake and eat, patrol, set up the gear, then wait and wait some more. Sometimes, she would wait for hours before firing a single calculated shot from her sniper rifle and ending a life. Then the team would return back to base. Every day seemed to be the same and she was getting tired of the killing. Even more so, she tired of the sitting, the waiting, the wasting away.

For Shoshanna Agnon, her career path had been one shaped by her father and, to some extent, her grandfather. With a Jewish father but born to a Syrian mother, she grew up not truly welcomed in the mosques or temples of either religion. To others, she belonged to neither faith and was often treated as an outsider. A daughter of a military family, her father and grandfather had served on the front line many times; their operations targeted and directed against the very faith of her mother. Yet, they did so for the benefit of their dominant male society and her Jewish homeland.

At sixteen, she was delivered to the door of the local national service office in her home town of Nazareth, and from that time onwards, she would rarely go a day without holding a weapon of some sort or taking orders and direction.

At eighteen, after two years of training and much bullying by the larger male soldiers, on occasion even enduring beatings, she passed out of military academy. Shoshanna was assigned to the Tzahal, the army for the defence of Israel. As a Syrian, her mother was not granted permission to attend the prestigious passing out service. Even her father and grandfather, while they did attend, stood at the back, a distance away, not associating themselves too much with their female family member, now a professional soldier. While moderately proud, they kept their distance so as not to tarnish their reputation amongst their fellow soldiers and veterans.

Both men had secretly wished for a boy. But since this was not delivered to them by her mother, they would often adopt a standoffish approach to her upbringing. Although they would never let her go short of anything, or without the very best on offer, they chose to do it from a distance. Shoshanna would receive the finest education and the safest home life. She was loved, although not openly by the male members of the family, and she was cared for. Her mother would often conduct the role of both her parents and do so willingly.

In her youth, Shoshanna would be left to fend for herself at school or on the streets and would often return home with bruises or items stolen. When out with the few female friends who would socialise with her, she inevitably came back distressed from the taunting and bullying. Her father would simply pass her on to her mother to deal with, for he could only see weakness in her tears.

Shoshanna's mother acted as both parents. She would be the shoulder to cry on and her safety net. She loved her mother very much and would often wish she could experience her maternal culture. But being born to a Jewish father, she was never going to be made welcome in Syria.

She would get to Syria several years later, but would find herself there as a special operator tasked with eliminating her mother's creed for the sake of her father's religion. Then she would find herself sitting and waiting, looking through the crosshairs of a sniper rifle, before her target appeared and their death would follow. It was not how she had imagined her time in her mother's homeland.

Her grandfather had served in the formative special forces Unit 101 in the 1950s, protecting the fledgling state of Israel. Her father would graduate into the Shaldag special forces years later. Shaldag was Israel's forward air control and reconnaissance unit, and it was from this time that the family started to show internal discord. Her father would be assigned covert operations inside Iraq to hunt down, and eliminate warlords hell-bent on sending evil across the desert and into his homeland. Often, this designated wickedness would come via Lebanon but more so through Palestine. He became very adept at merging into these societies while he hunted his prey.

Her father could be away for weeks without any communication. Then, on each visit home, instead of spending catch-up time with his direct family, he chose to be with his closest friends – his military family. The men would spend hours on the deck speaking about how many Sunni Muslims he had eliminated. He always longed to go back to kill more; it was in his blood, and he felt more at ease with the tension and killing than the caring and sharing of his domestic world. All the time, Shoshanna's Sunni mother would listen to their stories of death but hold her silence and simply cook their food. That was her place. It was the way of a woman in a male-orientated Jewish community and she never forgot the bond of loyalty she owed her husband.

Time passed quickly during her training, and Shoshanna got better and better in her role. She was promoted many times and after much encouragement from her commanders, she stood on the brink of qualifying into the most elite of all her nation's special forces units – the recently formed Shayetet 13. 'Shayetet 13' meant 'never again' and was the pinnacle of the country's fighting forces. It was designed simply to maintain Israel as a free and independent state, at any cost and with any sacrifice.

She would often be seen first on the training ground and last to leave. Most of her male colleagues wondered when she slept but, of course, Shoshanna never really did. Long ago, her mind and her body had made a deal together, and the result was that she could operate at the highest levels, in the hardest of conditions, without a regular need for rest. This most unusual ability would carry forward, away from the training parade, and onwards through her military career and beyond.

Shoshanna excelled all through the twenty-month intense 'boot camp' period. Most fellow recruits simply could not keep up with her. When some colleagues had finished advanced weapon training drills, maritime warfare exercises, parachute jumps or the long-endurance swims, she would return to 'the start' and go again.

Nearing the end of her Shayetet training, Shoshanna earned herself the chance of leading a group of other recruits in specialist counter terrorism – concealment – and sniper-training.

She had risen above the best of the best and was ready for whatever her enemies threw at her, or what her country demanded.

On her graduation day, her father stayed close to her. He stood front and centre, as he watched his little girl become the first active female operator of this formative and secret unit, which would go on to eclipse everything that he had done in his military career. Now she had proven herself to be as good as a man, he could stand full of admiration and pride. On the occasions that their eyes met, he would smile back.

Shoshanna's grandfather had died a few months earlier and, as Syrians were not allowed on the base, her father now stood alone to watch the graduation. Meanwhile, Shoshanna's mother sat on the porch back at home, waiting for their return. While proud of her daughter's achievements, she would often wonder why she had received this destiny of raising a military family. One that would see her child become a killing machine, or worse, killed in the line of duty, leaving her prematurely.

The dinner that night, back at the family home, would be an event that all would remember. Her father had spared no expense sourcing the best produce the markets around Nazareth had to offer. He had invited all his friends round to show off his trophy daughter; he even expected members from his former unit to appear. He hoped that they would talk with her, and share their experience and advice, as he did, before she received her first special-operations posting.

Her mother would cook for them as she always did and would listen to them in silence from inside the house. Wanting so much to take her place at the dinner table and be a simple family, she knew that her husband's friends would frown upon it and that her place was to provide food without any further interaction.

His former unit members knew that Elazar Agnon was married to a Sunni Muslim, but none would raise it this night. Nor would they expect to see her at the dinner. After all, this was an observance of being Jewish, a celebration of will and strength, and one for their good friend to savour. It was not one to be ruined by the presence of a faith whose sole purpose was to destroy everything that they stood for.

From the kitchen, hot and a little tired, she heard the jeep engine getting louder as it got closer. She knew it was her daughter, her lovely daughter who, while arriving now, would soon leave her for places where death and deceit thrived. She would be sent to areas that her government and her husband could not speak of. Yet, for now, her wonderful daughter was coming home and her heart beat a little faster, on this occasion with joy, not trepidation.

Shoshana's mother sat for a moment and smiled to herself, for there was no one else allowed in the kitchen to smile to. She had no help to prepare the feast for her daughter's celebration. The men would likely take over this joyous moment anyway. She sat and she smiled. She was a proud mother and she hoped she would remain this way for many years to come – with a beautiful living daughter.

An hour passed and the celebration was in full swing. The men sang their songs and they ate the food presented to them. They all celebrated Elazar's success. He had brought Shoshanna up to be the next line of defence for their great nation state. More so, he had brought her up to go to hell on earth to do a job. To protect her country. Truly, Elazar had done well and the men would celebrate long into the night.

Shoshanna sat with them, eating and drinking in moderation, but pleaded fatigue when they tried to raise her to dance with them around the barrel fire, now sending sparks and flames upwards into the darkened night sky.

"Sho, why do you leave the party?" her father asked, now a little worse for wear with locally made wine.

"I need to radio into command, Father," she said. What she really wanted to do was steal some time to speak with her mother, knowing her father would not fully agree with this in the presence of all his friends.

"Yes, my precious daughter, ever the soldier. Do as you must, my sweet, and quickly return to us here. We have much still to celebrate," he said. She turned and walked into the house.

Shoshanna pushed the kitchen door open. "Mother," she said, as she entered the kitchen unannounced. As her name left Shoshanna's mouth, her mother burst into tears and collapsed a little in relief, only to be grabbed and supported by her daughter.

"Mother, I am back. I am here for you, my loyal mother," she said, as she helped the crying woman onto a chair by the table.

"Shoshanna, you should not be in here while they are outside. They will not like you to be with me at your father's celebration. You must leave. I have food to prepare."

"It is my celebration and I do as I please. I choose to be with my mother right now," she replied. Shoshanna knew the sacrifices her mother had accepted to make sure that she received the best upbringing, shielded from her father's rage when it surfaced.

"Sho, you must do as I ask, my special girl. Go join the men," her mother pleaded, trying to shepherd her daughter back outside.

"Mother, I am staying for a while. Sit, please, sit with me. Let's talk," she commanded as she pulled up a second chair next to her and sat down.

Her mother remained seated as instructed. She secretly wanted to sit. She secretly wanted to speak with her 'little girl' whom she suspected could be whisked away at a moment's notice by the government.

"So," she started, her hand on her daughter's lap. "Do you have a boyfriend yet?" It was a wishful comment and an obvious opening, but, sadly, one that she suspected she knew the answer to.

"My mother, you already know that answer. I am already married. I am married to the Shayetet, as daddy was and granddad before him. It's our way," she replied. Shoshanna knew her mother had so much more on her mind.

"And do you enjoy your job?" she asked, again knowing it was a pointless question. "Do you get to see and travel much?" came next. She was trying to be a mother but knew that this was no ordinary family relationship and that she was the mother of no ordinary little girl.

"Again, you know the reply. I cannot answer those questions, Mother." Moving the conversation towards easier topics: "How are you and how are you two getting on these days?" Shoshanna asked, placing a second hand on her mother's lap and looking her in the eye with a smile.

"We talk more now, often without anger. Your father grows old too slowly, I'm afraid. He still thinks he is the guardian of Israel."

"I know, Mother, it must be hard. Perhaps, be more patient? I could talk to him…"

But before she could finish, she was interrupted.

"No, you must never mention this conversation. He would feel betrayed. Please tell me you will never mention this to him. Tell me," she said in a firm parent-to-child tone.

"Yes, Mother, relax, I will say nothing."

As her mother sat back in her chair, momentarily more relaxed and reassured, she thought she saw the kitchen door move slightly. Her head turned towards it. Was it the wind?

"Mother, what is wrong?" asked Shoshanna, noticing her demeanour change.

"Nothing, dear. Now go back outside, your father will be waiting." Shoshanna stood and did as she was instructed. Kissing her mother on the hand, she turned to re-join the men in the garden. Although it was her achievements the men were meant to be celebrating, she mainly found herself listening to her father and his friends talking of their past adventures. As she did, her mind started to play games. Flash memories of her dark past came and went. Each time, she would noticeably exhale uncomfortably, and try to banish the memories back to her deepest and most hidden past.

It would be a few more hours before the early rays of the sun announced the arrival of the next day, yet, it would still be a while before the men would turn in and end the celebration. Shoshanna had left them to it earlier, trying to grab some much-needed rest and would sleep for a while longer before the sun's rays hit her face through the crack in her curtains. Her mother, meanwhile, spent the dawn hours alone in the warm air of the kitchen, keeping a distance until she sensed there were needs to be catered for. With the last of the guests gone, Shoshanna's father finally staggered into the house and collapsed into his bed. For that moment, he was a happy man.

Her mother would sleep on the sofa, now that the spare room was occupied by a loud, snoring Elazar Agnon. As the faint growl of the taxi disappeared into the distance, silence returned. For now, it was just the three of them. It had been a while since they were all three together. It would not be long before Shoshanna would leave her parents again and normal life would resume for the remaining two.

But for the next few hours after rising to start the day, they would enjoy each other's company. It was easier for him to enjoy his daughter's presence when his friends were not there. He was even a husband on occasions, when his friends were not around, and this morning, he sat next to his wife and held her hand as they all spoke.

"My lovely girls. What a great night we all had," he exclaimed as he sat at the table and waited for his breakfast.

Elazar could be kind and fatherly at times. This morning was to be one of these occasions.

The three would sit and laugh. They would look at old black and white photographs of Shoshanna as a baby. The photographs were paraded in front of her, one at a time and she would smile as she watched her parents describe happier times. Faith did not interfere with these moments in the Agnon household, but these moments of happiness were too few and too far apart.

When her secure phone rang a while later, the happiness was brought to an abrupt halt, the smiles rapidly fading. They all knew exactly what was about to happen and no amount of preparation could ever hide the emotion that always burst free when she got the call. Her mother remembered the many occasions that the ringing of a phone would take her husband away for weeks and now it was the turn of her daughter – her precious little innocent girl.

Shoshanna's mother instinctively put a hand across her mouth to hide her expression.

Her father stood and watched her, as if he were the one receiving an order.

Buzzing phone in hand, Shoshanna looked at them both before rising to her feet and walking a short way across the garden. She accepted the call.

For her parents, the moment seemed to last an eternity, but it was a mere sixty seconds. They didn't speak in that everlasting minute, nor did they take their eyes off their daughter discussing her destiny down the line of her secure phone.

When she ended the call, Shoshanna returned to her parents. One had already accepted she was leaving them; the other tried hard to deny it.

"So, my love, what shall we cook together for lunch?" her mother asked in hope. The answer was not one that automatically followed on logically.

"Rations and airline food for me, Mother. I'm leaving now. I must pack my stuff and await transport." Finishing her sentence with a gentle hand on her mother's shoulder, but not stopping for a reply, she walked away from them and back into the house. None of them knew that this was to be her last ever time in the family home.

It would be two hours later when the noise of the rotary engine filled their street. The children ran shouting and jumping with excitement out of their houses. The sight of a military helicopter was a normal occurrence for children growing up in a state surrounded by enemies wanting and waiting to destroy them, but this occasion seemed a little different.

The helicopter hovered very low and waited, the dust from the street bellowing into the smiling and inquisitive faces of the children below. The branches of the trees swung more vigorously in the downdraft as the massive machine manoeuvred into position to land in a nearby concrete play park.

Shoshanna's father walked out of the house and over to the centre of the neighbouring playground, and guided the pilot slowly down. As he waved the helicopter down, the pilot acknowledged his signals and descended slowly towards the ground.

The two women walked out of the house, their arms around each other. Both wanted to show emotion but they knew they were not allowed to. He would not permit it. God-Country-Family, in that order and emotion merely placed family further down the order than it needed to be. It was his way and had been subconsciously enforced upon them. This was about lifestyle, one they had chosen to accept and live with.

The helicopter landed where instructed by Elazar and two soldiers climbed down. They knew him and engaged in conversation as best they could above the noise of the rotary blades.

Elazar looked over at his daughter and nodded. It was time for her to leave. She had her tasking and she was to travel immediately back to her base. She would do as her father and country asked on this day. As she did every day.

"Know that I love you and know that I will see you again, my precious mother," said Shoshanna as she kissed her gently on the cheek and started to walk away. Turning a little and stopping for a second, she continued, "But also, should God not wish this to be so, know that I am grateful for all you have done for me. I saw everything you did for me and appreciate it all." Then, placing a finger gently across her mouth to signal she wanted no reply, Shoshanna uncoupled the lingering grasp of their hands and walked towards the helicopter.

When she reached her father, she noticed the two soldiers salute her. She acknowledged their actions but had something more important to do.

"Take care of her. You know, Father, that she is a good woman. I don't like it how you treat her when your friends are round," she said, confidently and firmly looking him in the eye.

He knew this moment had been coming; he knew his little girl was now a grown-up soldier. Perhaps, she would become an even greater soldier than he ever was. He listened, all the time knowing he could be looking into his daughter's eyes for the very last time. He did not want her to step into that helicopter with any remorse, so he listened patiently and accepted.

"When you chose to save her, Father, from the Shias mob, you did so because you cared about human life. You brought her here to this community and your world because you grew to care about her, and you both fell in love. Father, do not forsake that love now. You need each other, remember that." As she stared into his eyes, she thought she may just have noticed the glimmer of a tear.

It was Elazar's turn to speak. "Keep your head down, your thoughts focused and your eyes sharp. You will do your country a great service. God is with you, my child. Now go. Leave," he said as he turned, gesturing to the pilot to ready himself for take-off.

Shoshanna hugged her father warmly and he reciprocated. Then, as instructed by him, she threw her kit bag into the arms of one of the soldiers inside the helicopter and, putting her other hand out to take the palm of the other soldier, she pulled herself up and into the awaiting helicopter.

Shoshanna chose not to glance back at her parents as the helicopter started to lift off the ground. Instead, she went to meet the pilots. It was her way of instantly getting into the soldiering mind-set which had always kept her alive in the past.

If she had looked back, she would have seen her father already walking to the house and her mother no longer at the front door. Instead, her mother had moved into the kitchen to start to prepare the evening meal. The routine had returned in that instance. Until, that was, her next visit, if indeed God would allow such a recurrence.

Quiet returned to her family home as the noise of the helicopter faded into the distant sky. Her father's former army colleagues had seen the chopper pass overhead and knew that it meant their friend, Elazar, had lost his daughter to a secret assignment. They would leave him with his thoughts for a few days.

By the time she landed, ninety minutes later, at the Ma'alul military base, Shoshanna's parents were already sitting down to eat. All talk of their daughter was banned from the dinner table. It would be a very quiet meal that night.

She had her posting. Her father would enquire as to where she was off to, by calling in a couple of favours. But, like many things, he would keep this from his wife.

A short few days later, Shoshanna would be travelling behind enemy lines and into Syria.

A small Syrian village in the north of the country was being systematically cleansed of Christians and Jews. In doing so, the evil that was Islamic Spear had triggered a nerve back in Tel Aviv.

This was to be her first posting, assigned to her new special forces unit.

Days would pass much slower for her mother now with her thoughts of Shoshanna and worries about her safety. Her father kept himself busy and distracted with his friends, sometimes on the golf course, sometimes returning home late from a bar. During this time, Shoshanna and her team would rehearse their drills constantly as well as spend hours on the firing range within the killing house of their training facility.

Nothing would be left to chance. She would train with a vast array of weaponry until muscle memory meant that she could clean, load and fire instinctively rather than deliberately. Even do so with her eyes closed. She would spend time in the gym, often lifting more weight than some of the men around her and when she did so, she would always let them know. As a woman in a testosterone-fuelled world, she could more than hold her own.

Whatever time she had left would be spent with her self-defence instructor. The Shayetet world was one completely engrossed in fighting and, with Krav Maga as their hand-to-hand combat system, they were a formidable force even without guns.

There would often be a couple of hours left in each day to refuel on food and sleep, but not always.

Then they were given the green light to go operationally live.

Whilst the two helicopters took off in the pitch darkness to deliver eight operators deep inside Syria and into the lion's den, Shoshanna's mother was lying awake, unable to find the comfort she so desperately sought in sleep. This was nothing new; thoughts of her daughter often prevented her from sleeping. However, on this night, her heart seemed to ache more than usual, the gnawing pain lingering inside her ribcage. She sat upright and clutched her chest. As she rubbed her hand over her breast, the sharper pain slowly dulled back to its ever-present ache. Many miles away over a foreign land, the whirring of the two helicopters similarly faded from the hearing of the ground crew at Ma'alul military base. Their deadly cargo carried off into the night.

The sun rose early the next day as if to say 'get up, get going' to Shoshanna and her team, but they were already awake and already dug in. They were ready for a long day of watching and recording, remaining out of the sight of evil killers. Killers with no semblance of humanity, better suited to a prehistoric age.

The next twenty-four hours would be the same as past surveillance operations and the same as those still to come. Sit tight and watch during the day, perhaps, try to snatch a few moments sleep and, at night, leave the relative security of their secret location, and wander amongst the sleeping villagers, those that were left, to assess the enemy's number and strength.

Back home, her mother also had to conduct her own covert missions in and around the town. Walking through the market and on public transport, it was clear to her that she was not welcome. Instead, she was treated with suspicion; a Syrian walking amongst them. Worse still, a Sunni Muslim, covered from head to foot in black. Hiding in plain sight was an impossible task. It challenged her on a daily basis, her religion forbidding her to wear anything other than her full-length garments.

This new day would begin a different routine from the many past. This day was to prove harder, a turning point, something of which no one could yet comprehend the magnitude. This day would ultimately trigger future events across continents and into the homes of families, who, like Shoshanna's mother, knew the hardships of military life.

The sun was setting over both women, many miles apart. As her mother started the long journey back on the bus, carrying heavy shopping bags, her daughter was readying the team for the initial assault.

Shoshanna lay motionless – from her vantage point, her telescopic weapon ready to eliminate each and every enemy that entered the crosshairs. All the time, she would avert her focus from her colleagues, who would conduct controlled terror and destruction against the enemies in the town below. Sometimes, they would join forces with key allies and conduct joint operations, but mostly, they worked alone. They preferred it that way, for they would often disagree with their Western and Russian counterparts' methods. Ruthless killers they all were, but murderers of women and children they were not. 'Just stopping the next generation of terrorists' would be their allies' justification. Perhaps so, but some wars had rules and that was disregarding them.

The hit-and-run operations had been ongoing for several days and were proving highly successful. They would need to evac back to safety to avoid the hunter packs that would, soon enough, figure out what was happening, and come after them in force and without mercy. The capture and execution of a special forces operator would be a massive propaganda coup.

When word had reached the commander back at the base that Shoshanna's mother had been killed, he chose not to tell her. He chose not to pull her from the operation, which still had forty-eight hours to run. He suspected that she would still carry out the task with ruthless efficiency. However, he was not prepared to take the risk that the communication could compromise their position, or worse, that she would lose focus.

In a busy suburb of Nazareth, the bus had been mostly full when a group of youths, returning from an army careers fair, enthused with readiness and pumped with testosterone, boarded the bus. They were ready for action, their minds full of military dreams. While they would experience combat soon enough, it was Shoshanna's mother who would feel the brunt of their mislead anger and anticipation before the bus had travelled much further.

Paying the ticket price, they walked on the bus and instantly spotted her. It wasn't hard for them to do so, clad as she was in the religious dress of an outsider's faith.

They walked the length of the bus to confront her. The driver was told not to stop while other passengers, immediately intimidated by this presence, sat head-down in their seats, fearing trouble and trying to remain unnoticed.

Now she sat amongst them, against her will, knowing she was in trouble. She sat in silence, motionless. Then, when one grabbed her shopping and tipped the bag over, making its contents run down between the seats of the moving bus, she knew she had to remain quiet and accept whatever her fate might be. It would soon pass, and she would go back to Elazar and explain that the market shelves were empty that day.

Elazar had often told her this intimidation could happen and not to react, not to speak, if it did. She abided his advice and, head down, tried to hide alone in her thoughts.

"Hey, woman, what you hiding under there?" said one.

"Yeah, why you wearing that shit on a hot day like this," laughed another.

"She could be hiding a 'vest'," said a third. This same youth carried on, the obvious leader of the pack. "Best we check and see, boys. Don't want no boom with all these lovely people on here, do we?" and he gestured to a fourth boy to grab her head gear.

From inside his protected cubicle, the driver shouted at them to leave her alone. A fifth youth walked up and banged a clenched fist on the reinforced window of his cab. The driver turned away, his eyes back to the road and drove as instructed.

The bell rang numerous times; the other passengers wanting to get off. One older woman struggled to her feet, seeing what was happening, and as the bus went along the bumpy road, she slowly made her way to the gang at the rear.

"עכשיו נזק לך עשתה לא היא לבד אותה להשאיר, הרבה כאן תראה", she demanded in her native tongue – *Look here, leave her alone, for she has done you no harm.*

"Best you sit back down, old lady. The road is bumpy and we don't want you to fall, do we?" Then, as the gang member forcibly grabbed her arm to lead her away, the second pulled the head scarf off Shoshanna's mother in a ruthless act of religious disrespect.

She screamed in shock and true fear. Elazar had said that some would aim to intimidate, but he never said any would dare to touch her.

The first youth, becoming a little uncomfortable with the growing level of disruption in the bus, kicked the rear emergency door handle and it flew open. *The bus will have to stop now*, he thought. He had followed his friends into the bullying, but now wanted out. By doing this, however, he had inadvertently become an accomplice in the murder of the innocent women his friends were taunting.

The gang leader and the remaining two youths who were standing over Shoshanna's mother saw the open door as an excellent way to scare the woman of Muslim faith who sat close to the exit.

Dragging her to the door, they laughed as she screamed out in fear.

A nearby passenger found the courage to speak and stood to face them, demanding an immediate end to their stupidity. As he did so, the bus hit a pothole and juddered badly, throwing all those on their feet off balance. The driver instinctively slammed on his brakes. But this led to the further disorientation of those on board. Shoshanna's mother fell, head first, out of the still-moving bus and onto the concrete road four feet below.

One of her tormentors tried but failed to grab her to safety; they were trying to hang on, themselves. The bus wheels screeched and swerved as it came to a ragged stop.

The initial fall had not killed her, but had knocked her unconscious. Mercifully, this would disguise the pain of the fatal collision – a truck moving in the opposite direction past the bus. As the front of wheels slammed into her body, she was thrown up into the air, falling back to earth and the concrete. The back wheels of the truck, unable to stop in such a short distance, ran her over as the driver skidded and braked as best as the dusty conditions would allow.

Many things were set in motion for Shoshanna, and her family in the moments after her mother's death on that road heading back to her home and her Jewish husband, Elazar.

When told of the accident, Shoshanna would inherently change; her mind-set betraying both her true character and her loyalty to her country. She would become a lone wolf assassin, but it would be some time before she saw this change in herself.

The hour-long taste of a career in the Israeli Defence Force for the youths on the bus was over, and they would now be made welcome for many months in a hardened jail, separated from family as much as the separation they had forced upon Elazar and Shoshanna.

Elazar would soon embark upon his own weary and depressed path to self-inflicted death. And through this, in time, his daughter would become parentless.

The Shayetet would lose both a former member and a rising star, but that would take some time to come about. For now, Shoshanna would carry on with her waiting and, when night fell, killing those of her mother's own faith. Then she would reposition to do it all over again the next night. This career soldier, one of the finest ever to graduate and a leader of men on hundreds of undercover operations, was now the enemy of her state. While she did not yet recognise this change, it would soon enough manifest itself in a manner most lethal.

Something inside Shoshanna changed that night. Her desire to kill those of her mother's religion, the enemy of her country, left her and instead, she became focused on killing those from the West. Those with no remorse for death or any care for innocents, just like her innocent mother had been shown no mercy by her killers. She would turn, turn against the concept of special forces across the world and against any person or organisation that chose, in safe retirement, to benefit commercially from their career and walk away comfortably from their past.

Chapter 2
Audience

When he stepped away from the lectern, the crowd rose to their feet as one. They applauded loudly and he smiled as he walked the stage, taking in the reward for his hour-long talk. Philadelphia had strong ties to the military; the audience was always going to be a loud, boisterous and supportive one for David Spencer, a highly decorated veteran, now a speaker and TV presenter.

For an hour, they had been mesmerised by his words and gestures. His past was one of ruthless precision and, to some in the auditorium, his talk would resonate with their childhood dreams of heroism and bravery. Some cheered while others clapped the tall, proud man in front of them who, now a little older, was more a participant of the fine-dining arena than the violence of the front line. This former soldier now lived on the privileged side of society and for most of his enraptured audience, it was a justifiable reward for his years of self-sacrifice.

His host walked onto the stage and hugged him warmly. Their hands clenched tightly. They had known each other for nearly thirty years and this pair, now sourcing revenue from speeches and agent fees, once had a less reliable line of income. Both men had spent days, weeks and months behind enemy lines all across the world. They had, on several occasions, risked their lives to save one another. With the crowd applauding and the imminent chants of 'USA' seconds away, the two men prepared to walk amongst their admirers and absorb the respect of this most ardent atmosphere.

As they stepped down among the crowd, the bulky minders struggled to fit between the rows of seats where their employers walked. Sometimes, the men would allow group photos on smartphones, while other times, they would simply stop and scrawl a signature across a programme. All the time the minders struggled to ensure they kept pace.

When a tannoy announcement asked the audience to retake their seats, some took it as notice that their meet and greet with their new heroes was drawing to a close. Without warning, several men rushed towards the two speakers, desperate to get that photograph or signature before they were whisked away to the tranquillity of their five-star hotel to count their money and growing fame.

As the surge reached the two friends, the minders finally got caught up and retook the initiative, controlling the enthusiastic audience, holding them back and now stationary. The inspired crowd was stopped in its tracks.

The two friends, now a little less enthused by the chanting and signature signing, saw that their audience base was becoming more and more unmanageable. Both men acknowledged the closest minder and his efforts, and returned quickly back through the crowd to the relative calm of the priority seating area and the celebrity ticket-holders who would use the association with special forcers operators as a means to raise their own television credentials.

When they reached the VIP section, both men were visibly calmer, their breathing regular once more. This time, they had returned to safety from enthused supporters rather than extremist terrorists, with their guns and suicide vests, and a deluded wish to meet seventy vestal virgins up high in the clouds.

The two men began their exit from the auditorium, passing polite row after row of celebrities and former military. Shaking hands, they again stopped, in this safer environment, to allow a fan to take a picture and claim they knew special forces. Their desire to be associated with the best of the best was obvious to all who cared. But the two men, a little fatigued, spent less time in front of cameras, and instead, shook hands and walked on.

When Spencer reached the end of the row and the stairs up to the side exit, his eyes were drawn to a woman, still seated, while those around her stood and faced him. She sat still, facing away towards the stage. He soon reached the seat directly behind her and she turned her head marginally. It was enough to facilitate her peripheral vision, but not enough for him to look her square in the face and to perhaps recognise her.

He continued past her, but now he wondered why she had not risen and why she seemed uninterested in the events in the auditorium. Did he know her? Had he met her before? Did she not like his speech?

For now, however, he continued to walk towards the exit and the waiting car. Reaching the passage out, he turned and gave one final acknowledgement to the paying audience. Then, smiling slightly at his success, he glanced back at the now vacant seat where the woman had been sitting a few moments before. It was only a matter of seconds later, but she had disappeared from sight. Thinking it was probably for the best and that he could now put that strange flash meeting out of his mind, he turned back towards the exit and walked out.

Former Navy Seal operative, David Spencer, turned to face his long-time friend, just out of sight of the crowd backstage and the two men shook hands, parting ways. Both were now several thousands of dollars richer. It had been a strange night, yet, a profitable one and now the car was waiting to take him to his hotel. In the morning, he would hop on a private jet to Washington DC and a closed-group meeting of military hierarchy, where his second revenue stream was to consult on technical arms requirements for future special forces operations abroad. His absence from that meeting would make the inner pages of the late editions the next day. But for now, blissfully unaware, everyone followed the pre-arranged schedule.

Spencer walked a short distance behind his female publicity agent, pulling out his phone from his inner pocket to review emails that had stacked up during his one-hour speech downtime. His pocket had vibrated several times with the receipt of new messages. He wondered if they would contain notification of his next high-earning presentation and where it might be.

He stopped for a second in the empty, dimly lit corridor leading to the fire escape exit and his car as he focused his attention on the first email.

As his head bent down to read the first of many emails, Spencer felt an annoying, tiny, but sharp pain in his throat. He coughed instinctively, but as he did so, no noise emerged from his mouth. As his hand rose to locate the pain, he felt the cold of a tiny needle jutting out of his larynx. He tried to call out to his agent, but while his mouth shaped the words 'hey, Kathryn', his ears heard no noise. His larynx was already going into paralysis.

The needle pushed into his throat had dispelled a liquid that instantaneously shut down his vocal chords, stopping him from making any spoken noise. This was her objective and she had caught him off guard.

The second strike would also serve its purpose well. The seven-inch serrated blade was pushed through his clothing towards the base of his back and entered his right kidney. As she pushed it in further, she turned the blade a little. Retracting quickly, she found the second kidney when the knife plunged back in. Again, she turned the blade, lodged in the organ and again, Spencer was unable to utter a sound. She turned her face away from the pungent smell of the escaping gas from his stalling organs.

Spencer's mouth screamed in pain but no noise exited through his vocal chords. He fell to his knees as he tried to support his body with one arm, the other reaching behind him in reaction to the closest wound. When his face hit the wooden floor with force, he felt no pain. His body was already shutting down. Pulling his arm back towards his face, he looked at the darkening red blood. The colour told him from experience that his kidneys were ruptured and that it was now too late. He had himself killed in this most silent and efficient manner many times and the irony was not lost on him.

Seconds later, he would bleed to death where he had fallen.

It was nearly an hour before the auditorium cleaner noticed her dull-white brush turn red in the semi-darkened light of the corridor. The killer had moved the dead body to the side, under a hanging curtain. The cleaner's brush became heavy as the bristles clogged up with drying blood, her shoes sticking more than usual to the carpet.

The minders had followed their instructions and training, and had left through different doors, while the driver had been told to drive round to the main entrance and wait.

The next day's local news channels would headline the murder of a former special forces operator from Afghanistan and numerous other theatres of war, while an obscurely positioned obituary would tell of the death of the same operator's publicity agent, found in a skip, on the street outside the theatre. She had her throat cut in what the police were calling an attempted robbery. Her purse was found a short distance away with credit cards and money missing, but the photo of her young son remained in pride of place.

A few days later, after forensics had turned up no clues at the murder scene, the local police would put a call out to the public for help. They would use the local press, TV and radio to help widen the search area. CCTV was also utilised in the search for a woman seen walking away from the street, having exited the side entrance of the auditorium around the time of the killings. The CCTV would prove inconclusive, as would the public plea, but Shoshanna already knew this.

Shoshanna forcibly emptied the contents of her stomach down into the toilet of the cheap motel she stayed in that night. While killing was something that came easy to her, she still felt an ache deep in her heart. She had killed a fellow special forces operator. One of her own kind. And that bothered her somewhat. She would get no sleep that night as she thought about her actions and then, of her mother. Her mother's image would drive her on, and in the morning, she knew she would feel better and plan the next operation with a focused mind.

"The second will be easier," she said out loud into the silence of her dingy motel room. Staring at her reflection in the bathroom mirror and as if to reinforce her resolve, she spoke out loud again, "Yes, second, easier." Then walked over to the small single bed with the stained mattress cover and closed her eyes as she hoped for sleep that night, having spent the rest of that day out of sight from general view. She would get no sleep however, for the images and the noises would soon come to play havoc in her mind.

Chapter 3
Sand

Shoshanna woke the next morning at around five am. A little surprised that she had managed some sleep, she sprung up out of the sagging excuse for a motel bed and walked into the bathroom. Her head was clear, once again, of any doubt or guilt from the night before. She was who she was and it didn't take killers long to move on. After all, Rock Spencer didn't seem to show any signs of remorse over deliberately razing two villages, and slaying the women and children living in them. He must have pulled off some story with his commanders, to get fast jets to completely obliterate innocents. *He didn't mention that in his many books or last night in his speech*, she thought to herself.

Switching on the shower tap, she took her t-shirt off and dropped her shorts to reveal her perfect muscular physique to the full-length mirror on the back of the door. When she looked over her former wounds, now scars, she saw the death and destruction she had herself caused. For others who were given the opportunity to look over her naked body, they would likely only feel desire. To those few that really knew her, mind and body amassed to a functional machine, always ready to exploit every sinew and every ounce of power to reach the goals set of it. This, for her targets, usually meant death.

She had a tattoo on the central lower part of her spine. A black circular-shaped symbol, which she got when she graduated from her Shayetet unit, many months ago. Every graduate had this; it was a Hebrew symbol meaning 'clenched fist'.

The most obvious blemish on her near perfectly shaped body was a nine-inch scar running down from her upper left shoulder and onto her breast. It had been self-inflicted, the night she heard of her mother's demise. It was her way of cleansing her anger. While this had worked at the time, now, in a cheap American motel room, the scar seemed to be failing its duty. The anger kept building inside her. She blamed her kind and her creed for her mother's death. As a result, she felt the untamed desire to become an avenging angel, ridding the world of ruthless and merciless killers. Others, in her wake, would only see her full of fury and rage. It would be their last vision before darkness fell.

Shoshanna showered and dressed, then spent a few moments checking, and then rechecking her two weapons and ammunition. A further few minutes would be spent sharpening her knife blade. She readied herself to leave the room and pressed an ear against the door to listen for any sound in the outside corridor. It was silent. In seconds, she had exited the motel without incident and, avoiding the CCTV at the reception, walked out into the busy street. It was the start of a new day and the beginning of the end for her next target.

Shoshanna disappeared into the crowd like a ghost. Avoiding street cameras as best as she was able, she reached the Greyhound bus station thirty minutes later and searched the boards, looking for the right destination.

She had changed clothing since leaving the motel and was now just another passenger wondering where to go to get to their transportation. Reviewing the timetable screens and the position of the CCTV inside the terminal, she carefully made her way to the departure location for her coach out of the city.

'Platform 4, 6.20am, Carson City, Nevada'.

The desert was an uncompromising and deadly place for the untrained. It was only marginally safer for the highly skilled former US Ranger, now TV adventurer, Mike Ridge. However, it was an environment he thrived in. With too many tours behind enemy lines to remember, Ridge had been dropped out of planes, dug into the dirt for days, risked broken bones floating like driftwood down rapids and climbed snow-peaked mountains with little more than a back-pack in his twenty-two-year career in the military.

Like many before him, he was utilising his past to create a good life, and comfortable homes for his family and their future. This day, together with a cameraman and a support-helicopter crew of two, Ridge was to risk life and limb filming the second, more adventurous part of his survival-school series.

The crew would spend ten days in the heat and remoteness of the north-eastern Nevada desert. Its population comprising only of snakes, pack animals and mosquitoes, all of which threatened deadly bites and blood-thickening pain. The helicopter would be the two men's last hope, should they succumb to the harsh environment, the closest hospital being over one hundred kilometres from where they would be dropped.

Shoshanna's bus journey was uneventful. She sat at the rear and tried to sleep against the emergency exit, her belongings pushed under her seat, where she could always feel them, rather than in the overhead storage. She tried to sleep but could not, her mind speeding faster than the bus she travelled on.

She watched the clouds and hills pass by her window, whilst her imagination was recalling evacuations by helicopter from burning mud villages or leaving the scene of combat by fast boat. In her mind's eye, she recalled leaving the ground at speed in a Black Hawk helicopter. She could see the horror that she had caused in their eyes as she flew off. Now, it was for others to deal with – those who had to stay and live in the villages with the memories of visiting death. She would never return to the scene of their battles ever again. Dark images occupied her thoughts in sharp contrast to the sunlit green hills passing by.

The LED display on the back of the seat in front of her read 'Carson City 3.45pm', still three hours away. Shoshanna rolled up her coat and, using it as a pillow, tried again to get some sleep.

The pilot went through his final pre-flight checks while the other three men sat and drank bottled water out on the concrete of the helipad. It was hot. It was always very hot. Nevada in summer knew nothing else, but this heat was why they chose the location. It was a deadly enemy against whom they would battle.

Within the hour, the three support crew, and Mike Ridge would be moving high and fast over the desert sand. The pilot would drop his cargo of former special forces operator and cameraman deep into the remote heat, and barren wastes of the desert. He would then fly on to the first rendezvous point and wait for them to arrive. The schedule said it would take Ridge and Peterson thirty-six hours to reach the first rendezvous point, but the reality was that no one really knew exactly how long it would take them.

The bus pulled into Carson City, the huge hydraulic brakes letting off a thankful hiss as it parked up to let people disembark. The vehicle's mechanical parts were under huge strain from the distance travelled and heat stress. The co-driver unlocked the side hatches, and started taking out large suitcases and backpacks, only to throw new ones in. The passenger complement changed as some left, and others waited to get on and find their seat. Next destination, Las Vegas.

Shoshanna had already exited the bus, mostly unnoticed, carrying her overnight bags, and walked the short distance to the main street and obscurity. When the driver counted heads prior to departure, her seat reservation would show 'Las Vegas'. But she would not return. She had paid to go the farther distance, yet, had deliberately disembarked early, at Carson City, hoping to avoid watchers and prying eyes at the final destination.

It was a simple enough trick, much like depressing a number of floor buttons in a hotel lift and not just the one holding the room reservation. It always seemed to work, throwing would-be interceptors off the scent. Fuelled by her anger, her paranoia was building. The two emotions would complement her skill set – complement her killing prowess.

For now, however, she presented the motorbike-rental man her fake ID and driving license, and, choosing a bike suitable for cross country, secured her two bags to the back of it. Around forty minutes after she had stepped off the bus, Shoshanna was once again on the move. This time, her journey would take her over the desert, rather than through it by road. Her initial target – a support helicopter and its two crew members. Social media was her friend. By 'following' her targets under a pseudonym, she got all the logistical arrangements she needed. The rest was easily established through research. The production company would happily reveal to the world the plans and filming schedule for their next series.

When Mike Ridge and his cameraman, Russell Peterson, wiped the sand and dust – blown up into the air as the helicopter had departed – from their goggles, both knew the bravado had ended and real-life survival had begun. Although they were anticipating some challenges, neither man could have possibly known that they would not see their support crew, friends and family ever again. Neither man could ever have imagined that a woman with body-length tattoos, an experienced assassin, was seeking them out.

They set off on their long march through the shimmering desert, to film their encounters with sidewinder snakes in the heat of the day and the packs of coyotes that would show interest in them in the cold of the night.

The first rendezvous point for the team to get back together again would be forty kilometres away and would take the helicopter less than thirty minutes to reach. There would be plenty of time for Shoshanna to take care of the two pilots and then start her secondary assault in the desert heat, on the two trekkers, who would be moving slowly on foot towards her.

The sun was setting over the desert when the first of two assassinations took place. Both killings were executed by a single shot to the head with emotionless professionalism. The bodies of the two pilots would lay where they fell, cold and still, waiting to be discovered for over two days.

Under the darkening sky and the building cold, Shoshanna worked on the helicopter. She didn't take long to permanently disable the flight systems and extract its GPS unit, before returning to the shelter and settling down for a short rest. The alarm now set, the bodies of her earlier handiwork were covered but still in sight from where she sat. The night predators would have to be very stealthy to gain access to the corpses, driven by the scent of death and blood. Still, they would wait patiently for their chance.

It was still dark when the noise of her motorbike exhaust startled the creatures of the desert. She would take the bike a short distance to a vantage point and hide it, to collect it after this specific operation had been completed.

The desert sand flew in all directions as the bike tires cut through the slopes and dunes, the dim light nevertheless obscuring the extent of her movements and her direction of travel.

At her planned target point, she cut the engine and got off the bike, laying it down into a slight depression in the sand. She set about covering the starting mechanism and gearbox with plastic wrap, to secure it against the sand, then after setting its GPS position into her watch, she started out on foot towards her targets. She would make contact soon enough, but for now, Shoshanna walked the hot sand, thinking about her mother and her lost life back home.

She missed her mother greatly. Each and every time she thought of her, a part of her still-beating heart died. She also wondered about her father. How was he coping without her mother? She could imagine him sitting alone on the deck, drinking and staring into the endless night. She had too much time to think. She longed for the pending contact and the distraction that it would bring.

The sun was rising higher into the sky and the heat would soon prove unbearable. She had limited the weaponry and rations that she carried to make the trek as easy as possible. Surprise would be her strongest weapon. She also suspected that her primary target would likely only carry a knife for skinning and eating whatever prey they caught. The kill should be an easy one.

The killing of another former special operator, however, was proving less easy in her mind. Her new reason to exist, turning against her erstwhile kin, meant that somewhere deep in her sub consciousness was a growing hatred of herself and her past, manifesting into a need to cleanse the world of these faceless assassins. She had seen special operators, herself included, engender too much evil under the banner of government and country, and it ate away at her.

"Mike, are we stopping soon? The camera's melting and I only have a few spare parts with me," said Peterson. He was struggling in the arid heat and while being used to carrying weight over tough terrains, the months following Ridge around the world were really starting to take their toll. "Mike, buddy, I really think we need to stop. The equipment's suffering *big time*," he emphasised.

"Equipment or you, old man?" came the terse reply. "We can't stop just anywhere, Russell. We need to be clever and find shade, remember? And I see none. Do you, mate?" Ridge questioned as he marched on relentlessly.

"Fuck off… Ok, I need to stop and drink water, Mike," Peterson begrudgingly conceded.

"Right then, my friend, now we have established the real reason, let's take ten," Ridge replied with a smile. "Get the temp sunshade up first, then take on some water. Oh, and don't tell me to fuck off again, or I might just fuck off and leave you alone out here in this oven of a desert," he said with a wry smile on his face.

The two desert walkers let their heavy backpacks fall to the hot surface and pushed the lightweight shade into the sand. It was large enough to provide temporary cover from the sun for both men. They sat on the sand and drank thirstily. Peterson also ate a chocolate bar, kept cool in the specially designed pouch in their equipment bag. Ridge had patented the design after devising its use in Syria while on operation. He would not live to exploit the massive revenue generated from the patent.

Ridge knew it was wrong to sit exposed in the desert heat for too long. He knew they needed to reach the series of dune depressions, still several hundred metres away. They would then be able to find an angle that would support their proper rest and recovery from the immense heat. He was also well aware that his long-time friend was not the strong and enduring cameraman he once used to be.

Ridge raised his GPS phone to the view of his friend so he would feel reassured and dialled in to the support helicopter.

"Desert Walkers to Air Horse, this is Desert Walkers, come in please," he said into the microphone.

Silence.

"Air Horse, this is Desert Walker, come in please, over," he repeated, in the same calm and controlled manner.

While he waited for a reply, fully expecting the phone to crackle into life at any moment, he gestured to Peterson to start packing up. They were heading on to the series of sheltered sand dunes ahead.

The silence became deafening.

"They better not be sleeping," Peterson eventually cut the quiet.

"Sleeping? No, I guess they've opened a beer and put us on hold," Ridge smiled back. "Anyway, my friend, let's crack on and try again when we hit slightly higher ground."

Peterson was slightly relieved by his friend's comments and lack of obvious concern over the radio silence. Ridge, however, knew a higher vantage point was meaningless. This was a GPS phone and the signal went straight upwards and into space. A sand dune was no great boon for the technology he now repositioned into the side of his backpack.

Ridge stared ahead at their target destination.

A few hairs rose on the back of his neck. The fingers on his right hand, his gun hand, twitched involuntarily.

Looking ahead over the heat haze, Ridge narrowed his eyes slightly to help him focus better.

"Buddy, I'm waiting, let's crack on," Peterson said. The words broke the silence and brought Ridge back to the present, back to the awareness of the heat that battled down against them both.

"Yup, right. On it," he said. "I just thought… em, nothing, Russ. Let's go." And with that, Ridge slapped a firm hand against the back of his friend and walked on.

Under the temporary shelter of the sunshade, the two men had briefly discussed the next filming opportunity and how it might pan out. It had crossed Ridge's mind, after the radio silence from the support helicopter, that it might be time to do a 'piece to camera'. After all, tension like this gave his show that watchable edge. But for now, the two simply walked as best they could, against the collapsing and shifting sand.

His voice had made her blood curdle. She had heard it before. They had both been in the same special forces reconnaissance unit in Syria and Ridge had been tasked with calling in airstrikes against a number of Sunni townships that they believed were harbouring Islamic Spear leadership. It seemed he had done this many times before.

Shoshanna had seen at close range the devastating effects of five hundred pound, laser-guided bombs on enemy and innocent alike. She had seen more than her fair share of body parts, both soldier and child.

Several hundred metres away, waiting for the desert walkers, she had listened to Ridge's voice attempting to contact the helicopter pilots' GPS phone. When he had called the support team, her blood boiled inside her veins. She was waiting and ready once again.

Capturing their exact location and direction of travel from that ill-fated call, Shoshanna now began to execute her plan with ruthless efficiency. She calculated she had sixty minutes until contact but would need much less time to be ready for him.

Ridge felt uncomfortable after the failed call to the support crew a short while earlier. It was time to try again and to dispel the nervous uncertainty he held in his gut. Suggesting that they abandon filming for the afternoon and instead get out of the heat, he reached into his rucksack for the phone. They would start again once the cooler night air descended and the reptiles came out to search for food. The cold of the desert night was as much a survival challenge as the daytime heat proved to be.

"Desert Walkers to Air Horse, come in, Air Horse."

"Is there a problem, Mike?" said Peterson.

Ridge ignored his friend's question.

"Guys, answer the fuckin' call," Ridge shouted at the phone. Then, realising that he may have over reacted, he turned to Peterson and smiled. "Guys must still be setting up or something," he said in a reassuring tone.

The wind was blowing sand and sound in a north-east direction. It carried their voices up and over the dune immediately in front of them. She didn't need to have her stolen GPS phone switched on to know they were close. In fact, she had switched it off, so as not to have her position compromised with any stray wavelength interference.

Ridge again felt uneasy. *This doesn't happen, it just doesn't*, he thought to himself. His training took over and a sense of 'hope for the best but expect the worst' kicked in. He started to consider options. *What could have happened? Have they crashed?* Was he overreacting?

Sensing something was wrong, he nodded to Peterson with a reassuring smile while putting the phone away and moving off up the dune.

When Peterson saw Ridge pull his hunting knife out from its protective sheath, he too started to feel uneasy.

What was his soldier friend's intention? Had he seen something that he himself had missed?

"Mike, you ok, buddy?" said Peterson, eyeing the serrated blade in his friend's hand.

Ridge responded immediately. "Sidewinders… snakes. They move down dunes fast, brother."

Both men knew this was a stupid excuse and not the real reason the former soldier had felt obliged to pull out a weapon, but it was accepted by Peterson for now and no further question followed.

The two men reached the summit of the dune and stopped to look out over towards the next. Peterson looked around for the right location and angle to pitch up the sunshade properly, and prepare a temporary resting place. Ridge was looking for something completely different.

"What do you think, Mike? That looks sensible," he said to his colleague, pointing to the base of the dune and a little over to their left where a shadow was trying to make a home. The sun was starting to get low and with it came shadows moving eerily across the sand, back and forth.

His colleague seemed not to hear him. Instead, Ridge was focusing all his senses on the downward slope in front of him. Hairs stood to attention all over his body and his heart pumped just a little faster. He closed his eyes, and focused his ears and his mind, tasking them with identifying the cause of his unease.

In his mind, he reviewed every detail his eyes had seen earlier. He held his breath to further assist his hearing. Peterson stared at his colleague, conscious not to move or distract him in any way. He had seen this before with Ridge. It had saved his life. Mike had stood on top of the Land Rover roof in Northern India once, while filming an earlier survival documentary. Suddenly, Mike had grabbed the rifle from the guide and fired three shots into the long grass. Seconds later, a tiger ran off, deciding that this time he wasn't hungry enough for the fight. Now, as Mike Ridge stood in the same statue-still pose, Peterson waited patiently.

Then he opened his eyes and focused his gaze on a small area of sand a few metres down the slope in front of them. Looking back at their own position, then back to the immediate vicinity of the original area of sand, he pointed to it using the shining blade of his knife.

"Russell, what do you see?" Ridge said, without taking his eyes off of the affected area of sand.

Peterson moved closer to his colleague and his eyes followed the direction of the outstretched blade.

"Look, buddy, down there at ten o'clock, nine metres," Ridge urged, the blade gleaming in the sweltering heat.

"I see nothing, Mike."

"Look, don't be a fuck. Have you learnt nothing over the years?" The atmosphere changed suddenly. Peterson became afraid, but not because of the aggressive demeanour of the special forces assassin next to him, but because his friend saw danger which he himself could not. Peterson focused.

"There, those ripples of sand. It's not like the others," he said. Without waiting for Ridge to respond, Peterson continued, now buoyed by his initial success. "They don't seem natural. They are out of place; they were not caused by our footsteps or an animal either."

Ridge interrupted, "And the wind direction?"

Peterson paused. "Fuck. They have been blown up the slope, against the wind. What the fuck?"

"Correct." Putting a firm hand out and onto his friend's shoulder, Ridge placed his rucksack down, and began to take a slow and wide approach round towards the suspicious area of sand dune.

Peterson watched as Ridge descended the slope, amazed at how he could do it with such little disruption to the sand beneath his feet.

Six metres. Four metres. Two metres now. Ridge crouched down. His blade slightly out in front of him. He waited. The waiting confused his friend back up the slope. Transfixed by what Ridge was doing, Peterson just stared. He couldn't move. He actually felt unable to move, such was his confusion and fascination. Then, anticipation quickly took him over.

Ridge gently dipped the tip of the blade into the sand in front of him and into the strangely configured ripples.

His actions reminded him of his past tours in Afghanistan. Moving his four-man team slowly through potential IED-filled roads and streets. This, however, was no improvised explosive device search. This time, Mike Ridge was probing for the unusual under the sand. His whole body and his inner being told him that something was wrong here, and with nothing on top on the sand, the dilemma must be under it.

He moved the point of the blade slowly in and out of the sand around him, searching for something, but he didn't know what yet.

When the sand behind his friend started to move of its own free will, Peterson could do nothing but stare. His gaze was transfixed on both his colleague crouched down on the sand and the slithering movement of more sand behind him. It seemed to be parting right in front of his eyes.

Then, "Mike, behind you!" he called out, but it was too late. She had triggered the trap and Ridge had fallen for the decoy.

Ridge snapped his head towards Peterson and saw the look of fear on his face. He grabbed his blade from the sand and turned around, his whole being now on fire with the sense of imminent danger, but it was too little too late.

The sand behind him did indeed come alive and like from a shallow grave, Shoshanna sprung at him. Incapacitating Ridge with a paralyzing neck hold with her right arm, she turned his face towards her. His brow furrowed as he recognised her, but only for a fleeting moment. With her free hand, she forced her own hunting knife into his closest eye. It went in with ease. She twisted the blade. He had not even seen the glint of metal racing towards his face and now it was too late.

With almost twenty years full service in the toughest of special forces, fighting the hardest battles day after day and night after night, he finally succumbed to his fate. A fate that was certainly not a war zone's, or even a sniper's bullet, but the setting of his own TV show.

Ridge's body fell limp in her grip just before she released him. He fell face-first onto the sand, his corpse leaving a red blood stain behind it as it slid slightly down the dune.

Shoshanna rose to her feet and pulled out a handgun. Without looking directly at where the body lay, she pulled the trigger, releasing one round into his back. The body failed to move as the bullet slammed into it and no doubt exited the other side, into the sand. He was already dead.

It had happened so fast that Peterson's petrified expression had not changed. Shoshanna looked up the slope towards him, into the face of a very fearful man.

She walked up the dune, her gun by her side, for she didn't expect to be challenged.

"Your camera!" she demanded.

Shaking, Peterson handed it over. Shoshanna opened the USB slot and took out the memory stick, breaking it in half.

"Are there others?" she asked, more calmly and methodically.

Peterson took off his shoulder bag and threw it to the sand by her feet. Kicking it open, she considered its contents, but decided to do nothing with them. Instead, she inserted the tip of her blade into the camera's housing, wiggling it back and forth, prying, breaking, opening its parts up to the light. Satisfied that she had damaged it sufficiently, she handed it back to Peterson. He instinctively took it back.

"Do you have water?" was her next question to him. Peterson had emotionally drifted away. His eyes looked back down towards his dead friend.

"Water!" she barked out at him, bringing him back to the present.

"Eh, yes, do you want some?" he replied haltingly as he took off his smaller backpack and, from within it, removed the large water bottle.

"Give it," she ordered. Opening the bottle, she turned it upside down in front of Peterson, and together, they stood and watched the water empty out and onto the sand. Almost immediately, it would evaporate and disappear.

"Do you want to live or do you want to end like him?" she asked, looking down at his dead friend.

Peterson lifted both hands above his head in a gesture of surrender, but as quickly as he did it, she struck one back down to his side with her gun.

"You have already surrendered, you fool. I said, do you want to live? It's a simple fuckin' question."

"Yes, live, yes." Peterson's brain struggled to process what was happening.

"Good choice," she replied, now a little sarcastically. "Go that way," she said, pointing the direction she wanted him to go. "If you're lucky and the coyotes don't get you first, you may make the nearest town. It's only thirty miles."

She gestured to him to start walking. He took a few steps as suggested, then turned and looked at her. He then looked down at the gun in her hand.

"I'm not planning to waste a bullet on you," she said. "Not unless you go towards him," Shoshanna gestured to Ridge's body. "Or on towards your helicopter team, both of whom are no longer able to help you, if you know what I mean."

Peterson knew exactly what she implied. She had obviously taken care of his support crew, as she had his close friend and now he was the sole survivor from the four-man team.

He turned in despair, after picking up his few belongings and started off in the direction instructed. He fully expected to hear the click of a gun being readied but it never came. Shoshanna watched Peterson walk into the distance, and, when he became lost in the heat haze, she turned and started back to her motorbike.

"Sad fuck," she said to herself out loud. "Thirty miles? Try three hundred..." And with a sinister smile on her face, she started to jog down the slope and quick march to her exit vehicle, using the GPS tracker and partly following her earlier footsteps, now disappearing into the moving sand.

Peterson would never be found. It would not be any rescue team that discovered his body. Instead, it would be several coyotes and they were all hungry.

Chapter 4
Journey

When the television production company reported their team missing in the desert, there were some who already suspected there was a wider problem. The crew's helicopter had been picked up by a surveillance satellite and it would soon be recovered by the incoming rescue team.

They would find more than they bargained for.

They would find two dead pilots and suspect that the other two were likely in real trouble. They would never establish the whereabouts of Ridge and Peterson; the packs of roaming animals would make sure of that. The desert was a vast expanse of moving and living sand, and remains were hidden quickly.

The discovery of the dead pilots, with the missing special forces soldier and cameraman, and the lack of communication back to the program sponsor, would create much chatter on social media and in the ex-service community around Ridge's family base in Houston. Social media would soon enough do its job and spread the word that one other former special forces soldier had recently died in mysterious circumstances, but as of yet, no one would place the last piece of the jigsaw into the puzzle. Shoshanna still had time and she would exploit it.

There were a lot of unknowns to put together for everyone involved, either directly or otherwise. It would take a while longer before the special forces community woke up to the fact that they were being attacked from within.

Elazar Agnon's friends would take a while longer to figure out that Shoshanna was unlikely to ever return to the family home. They would take longer yet to suspect and accept that she was involved in the unfolding events, and that she had betrayed her unit, her country and ultimately, the principles instilled in her by her now dead parents.

On the other side of the country from where the most recent former operative had met his untimely end, some had started to wonder if the deaths of these two Navy Seals were related. Rock Spencer's military community had had more time to reflect and to consider a conspiracy theory. They had pushed the local law enforcement to assign a greater amount of resources and time to their investigation. Some had escalated their concerns to their former unit commanders and this would have mixed results in the future. For now, however, the two former operators' murders remained conversational topics, open to debate, and for the news channels and papers to report on.

Shoshanna took her time travelling across Ukraine, en route to her next self-assigned mission in Kazakhstan. Landing in Kiev, she sat alone in the train carriage as it pulled out of the station and began its sixteen-hour journey to Lugansk on the eastern border with Russia. Sitting there alone, she finally felt safe enough to relax. She would be meeting Artum Bohdan, but for now, she rested and soon enough drifted off to sleep.

The train journey passed through the countryside incident free.

The same could not be said for Shoshanna's soul. Whilst body slept, her mind was very much alive with the sights and sounds of her past. Whether it was because her subconscious knew she was heading back to meet 'him' or it was simply coincidence, her nightmare didn't discriminate.

She saw him clearly, pulling the pin and throwing the incendiary device into the room, bolting the door after him. She saw him walk away and make a call on his phone, seemingly oblivious to the screams of children burning alive inside. The words he said to her as he walked past haunted Shoshanna for months after.

"Отойди красивая девушка. Все они вырастают террористы в любом случае." – *Come away, pretty girl. They all grow up terrorists anyway.*

She had hated working with the Russian Spetsnaz on collaborative anti-terrorist operations; these people were not human – they were cold, emotionless killers. She too was a killer, but somehow, she managed to convince herself it was for the greater good. Operating undercover with her Russian colleagues, however, had started to take its toll on Shoshanna. A cold, evil heart was forming beneath her calculating exterior, yet, at that time, many months and years back, she was not aware of its growing presence.

She remained almost motionless on the slow train journey across the Ukraine, but inside her head, she saw the raging flames and could recall once again the horror of the burning bodies. She could see the face of one teenage girl, now almost dead, her hands melted onto the bars of the window. And the smell, that smell of burning flesh would also stay with Shoshanna until she herself descended into hell for the crimes she had committed and was still planning to execute.

She was spared further torment as the ticket inspector placed a gentle hand on her shoulder to wake her.

"Мадам, будь ласка, чи можу я бачити…" – *Madam, please may I see…*

However, before he could finish his sentence, he found himself on the carriage floor with his arm uncomfortably held behind his back, and a rather groggy and angry woman applying pressure to his shoulder with her knee. She never slept really, even when her eyes closed and her mind wandered off. She was always expecting and waiting for danger, her body quick to spring to response.

Quickly realising her mistake, she released the hold and lifted the pressure from the train employee so he could breathe easily again.

"Яка халепа, мені дуже шкода, мій друг. У мене був дуже поганий сон. Страждають ви? Чи є що я можу зробити, щоб допомогти?" – *Sorry, sorry, I am so sorry, my friend. I was having a very bad dream. Are you hurt? Is there anything I can do to help?* – she said to him, realising in that instant that she needed to speak Ukrainian.

She was travelling on one of her many fake passports; her cover was that of a former Ukrainian police officer. Interpol could track passports worldwide, so she needed to move freely from America to the Ukraine without her trail being discovered on some desk assistant's computer.

Shaking himself down rather bemusedly, the ticket inspector simply returned to his original question.

"Мадам, будь ласка, чи можу я побачити ваш квиток, будь ласка?" – *Madam, please may I see your ticket?*

With the inspection now over, Shoshanna returned to her seat alone in the carriage. She suspected that she was now the topic of conversation amongst other train employees and it made her a little uncomfortable. She didn't like attracting attention to herself. Would there be police waiting for her at the next station? She shuffled down into her seat further but there was no more comfort to be had. She stayed awake and waited to see what would happen when the train stopped next.

Around an hour later, when the train pulled away from the scheduled stop and she had seen no uniforms board, she smiled at her good luck. He had not reported her, not seeming to have taken the incident any further.

She had six more hours on the train before she met her contact, Bohdan, who would escort her through Russia, and into Kazakhstan and onwards to meet 'him' once again.

She thought about how she first met Bohdan – he could not be trusted. No doubt, he would sell her out for a higher price if the offer came, but she needed him. His contacts and knowledge of the seedy underground-fighting world would make him valuable to her. That said, from the first instance they met – rescuing him on operation, tied, bound and half beaten to death, from the hands of Chechnya terrorists – she felt compelled to remain in contact with him. He had the ear of many influential people and her unit could benefit from the access. However, he was motivated by money only and he could never be trusted.

Right now, she needed food, so she made the long journey through the moving carriages towards the front and a rather antiquated restaurant car.

The car was dark and cold. There were candles on each table and flickering lights around the walls, with each bulb seemingly on the brink of extinction. It made the place feel like a scene from some colourless black and white film. The waiter approached Shoshanna with a menu but she already knew what she wanted: the hot borsch soup.

A short while later, after a second bowl, she paid and began to leave, when she saw the same ticket inspector from earlier walk into the dining car. She held the door for him and smiled. He duly smiled back, clearly not fazed by her earlier actions.

Strange, but lucky, she thought to herself. Starting the long, gently rocking walk back to her carriage, she smiled as she wondered if being attacked was a common occurrence for Ukrainian ticket inspectors.

As the sun was beginning to sink behind the hills and a chill crept its way into the train, Shoshanna knew it was not long now until they reached Lugansk. She had instructed Bohdan to meet her by the ticket office inside the rail terminal. But she had no intention of simply walking up to him and restarting their friendship – a friendship that had come to a sudden end after he had failed to show up on a reconnaissance operation during the Soviet invasion of the Crimea a few years earlier. Instead, when the train came to a halt and the steam from the rear engine filled the carriages, as they always did, she leapt off and crossed the tracks onto the next platform. Following the wall as close as she could, she disappeared into the crowd of passengers awaiting the next train out of Lugansk.

Comfortable that she was not seen or followed, she made her way to a vantage point a hundred yards from the ticket office and waited. She saw Bohdan straight away and, sure enough, he was visually filtering the hundreds of passengers coming down the platform from her train. She waited, and watched both her contact and others in the station for any signs of unusual activity, her hand never releasing its grip on her cleverly concealed gun with its safety catch already off.

Twenty minutes passed, and Bohdan was becoming more and more unsettled. He had expected Shoshanna to turn up promptly and not to keep him waiting. He turned his mobile phone around in his hand and wondered about calling her. His other hand remained inside his coat pocket. She wondered what he held in it.

Deciding to wait until his inevitable call came, she changed position and found a more comfortable spot from which to watch. Then, just as she had sat down, Bohdan started typing on his phone. Suspecting the call, Shoshanna had turned the ring tone to silent so as not to alert others to her position.

As she accepted the call when it came, she didn't speak.

"Agnon, where are you?" he asked.

Shoshanna remained quiet, watching him from a distance.

"Agnon, are you here? The train… oh, I see, you're watching me, aren't you?" he said with dawning realisation. As he turned around to look behind him, Shoshanna lifted the phone to her mouth. He scanned the terminal. She spoke.

"Bohdan, your standards are slipping. I have been watching you for twenty minutes now," she chastised. Not waiting for his next words, she spoke again. "I am right in front of you. The old Bohdan would have known that. We hide in plain sight and are always where we are least expected."

Swivelling around again, he responded, now looking directly towards her hiding place: "South-west corner, above the flower seller. Fine, game over. Come down, I am alone. Why would I betray you, Agnon? I expect you to earn me lots of money when you meet him," he said. She was already heading towards him, certain that he was indeed operating on his own.

"Bohdan, you look old," she said, not offering her hand in friendship.

"And you, Agnon, you look tired. Still having the nightmares?" he replied, offering his hand to his once friend and former special forces colleague.

Not appreciating his comment or the truth behind it, she walked off in the direction of the terminal exit. "Coming?" she asked, only half turning her head in gesture.

The next phase of her latest quest had started. She threw her two rucksacks into the back of Bohdan's jeep, and conceded to herself that she was again facing a long and dull journey on her way to Kazakhstan. This time, however, she wasn't alone and, unexpectedly, she liked that.

The jeep battled the battered road for hours. They passed through several checkpoints guarded by twitchy Russian soldiers waiting for the next attack from Ukrainian rebels seeking the return of their lost homeland. Each and every time they approached a checkpoint, Bohdan would reassure his passenger and climb down from the vehicle.

He would speak to the guards just out of hearing and when they all looked back at the jeep, Shoshanna grasped her handgun tighter. Bohdan would reach into his inside coat pocket and then shake the hand of the closest guard, surreptitiously delivering several notes, before returning to the jeep with a smile on his face. This continued through the night. Shoshanna fought with her desire to sleep and he would simply drive. They rarely spoke to each other but just stared into the distance, both looking forward to this journey's end and the start of the next part.

In the darkness of the jeep and with the night sky all around, Shoshanna eventually gave in to her body's fatigue. She didn't know when and for how long she slept. Periodically, her head banged against the side window but not enough to wake her.

When she did open her eyes, she panicked. "Fuck, I slept. How long was I out for? Where are we? What have you done, Bohdan?" came flying out her mouth as she momentarily struggled to process the situation.

"Chill, Agnon, it is just us. I didn't touch you; you're not my type," he said with a grin. "And, we are almost there. You must have needed the sleep. Now you are refreshed, it will be easy for you to beat him, yes?"

"Right, good, I hate this. I need to get out and stretch my legs, and, yes, if you had touched me, you would no longer be able to drive, Bohdan. In fact, you would no longer be able to breathe," she said, trying to regain the upper hand. She was annoyed for letting herself be at this man's mercy while she slept – her former friend, who she was slowly beginning to trust again.

"Beat him? That's just the start of it," she finally answered.

One hour later, as the sun had started to rise, they entered Kazakhstan. He was getting much closer now.

Chapter 5
Cage

Bohdan reached into his pocket and pulled out a number of notes of the local currency from his wallet, and passed them to the man on the door. Glancing down at the bundle of bills, the man pushed the entrance open. Shoshanna followed Bohdan inside.

When the door slammed shut, Bohdan turned to her and spoke in a quiet voice.

"No turning back now, Agnon."

"I never turn back," she replied quickly, not caring if anyone heard.

A second man stood by a different door and called them over towards him. After looking at them both and speaking into a shoulder-fixed radio, he directed them inside. They followed as instructed.

The room they entered was as bare of any furniture as it was appeal.

Throwing a rucksack onto the ground in front of a simple bench, Shoshanna surveyed her surroundings. Bohdan went towards the one small internal window, while she tugged at the door handle of what appeared to be to an adjoining room. When it opened, she froze for a second. She had expected it to be locked and was surprised that it simply gave way. She stepped forward through the doorway and into a long corridor, with the now curious Bohdan right behind her.

As they walked the dimly lit hallway, they became increasingly aware of the noise of rowdy and probably troublesome men. There seemed to be lots of them, all directing their focus and anger at one unifying source.

Shoshanna approached a new door and attempted to open it. The raucous din was coming from somewhere beyond. What they saw surprised both of them. As the door opened and the noise became deafening, they saw her imminent future.

The arena in front of them comprised a circle of dirt and gravel which, from their viewpoint, seemed to be ring-fenced with barbed wire, creating a round, roofless cage. Small wooden chairs were positioned just outside the circle, both accommodating a dirty towel, seemingly blood stained. There was a bucket of water and a sponge nearby each chair, and nothing more. Inside the makeshift cage, two men were grappling while a third stood and watched closely.

"Animals," said Bohdan as he looked around the crowd, each and every face anticipating blood. The two men inside the ring would cry out in pain occasionally as the other landed a punch, or gouged, pulled and twisted at parts of the body. The third man, acting as some sort of useless referee, would do little but push the losing fighter closer to the winning one to ensure the aggressive and noisy crowd got what they expected.

Money was changing hands at a rapid rate, with one Chinese man appearing to act as a bookmaker, shouting names and numbers, and collecting handfuls of notes as he did so.

"So you see what you have in front of you, my friend," said Bohdan, nodding in the direction of the circus.

"I have seen worse, Bohdan, done worse also," Shoshanna replied.

"No doubt, I will be winning a lot of money from your efforts," he said with a smile on his face.

"No doubt, you will. Let's go closer and look for him," she instructed.

"Will he not recognise you and know you are his fight if he sees you?" Bohdan questioned.

As Shoshanna walked the steps down, she replied, "Vitschencko never saw my face on that mission. He saw a woman in a black mask in the dusk light. He never saw me, but I saw him. I saw him for what he is and what his unit was." With Bohdan following close behind so that he could hear her words above the vicious, bloodthirsty crowd, she stopped and turned to face him. "He is one of them," she said as she jerked a thumb at the crowd. "He needs blood and screaming to excite him. He needs to live amongst death and better still for him if he can cause it."

Bohdan remained quiet, turning his gaze back to the crowd.

"Tonight, he will live amongst death forever, in hell," said Shoshanna, ending the conversation. Bohdan surprised her by placing a reassuring hand on her shoulder, which was quickly rejected.

"This is no place for sentiment. You have completed your job by bringing me to him. Whatever you get out of this is yours to have, Bohdan." She turned and went closer, down the stairs, towards the cage. Now yards away from the fight, Shoshanna could clearly see one occupant being dragged out, unable to walk but probably still conscious. His limp body left a blood trail in the mud and sand as he was disposed of. As the victorious fighter left soon after, bellowing out adrenaline-fuelled abuse at his defeated opponent, another man entered, and started throwing down fresh sand to cover the blood and sweat.

Shoshanna surveyed the now quieter crowd. She wasn't sure exactly what she was looking for, but she took in each and every face. None stood out to her; she recognised no one.

"Agnon, we are being called," came a shout from behind her. The man who had shown them to the first room earlier had approached again. Shoshanna turned and saw the large, imposing figure instructing Bohdan. Her colleague was looking a little intimidated but trying to put on a brave face.

"We need to get you to the back room to get ready. Seems you're on after the next fight," Bohdan said, trying to appease the unwelcome shadow standing over his shoulder.

"Right, settle, Bohdan, I'm coming now," she replied and, walking past her colleague to start back up the stairs, she spoke again. "I really don't like your boyfriend, Bohdan. He's one ugly fuck."

Even before entering the ring, Shoshanna's fight had started. She had begun to focus her mind on the task at hand and now everyone was the enemy.

The next hour was spent with Bohdan. For half an hour, he assisted her, taping up knuckles and wrists, helping her stretch and grease up. Then, as the fight approached, the last half hour passed with Shoshanna sitting in the corner, eyes closed, in what he thought was a type of meditation.

He would periodically speak to her.

"Agnon, are you sleeping?"

But she would ignore him or simply give him a stare that he correctly interpreted as an instruction to leave her alone.

When the door eventually swung open, Bohdan's shadow from earlier stood dominating the entrance.

"Now it is your turn to lose, bitch," he said, as Bohdan sprung, surprised, to his feet. "I hope he takes your face off, woman. It's what he tends to do, the Russian," said the large man at the door, with barely concealed glee.

Shoshanna stood and stretched. She wasn't worried by his comments. Bohdan and the stranger watched her walk over towards him.

"Move, ugly, or you will lose *your* face," she said and without waiting, she pushed him aside as she stepped through the door towards her fate. The man sneered in reply.

Bohdan followed close behind her and reached an arm to her shoulder. "Agnon, listen, woman, I know you will win but don't play games. Do what you've got to do and get out. Whatever he has done before doesn't matter. Keep that face safe and get me my money, quick."

"Bohdan, you are a sentimental old fool. I am a woman; I do as I please." She gently took his hand off her shoulder and pointed to an area where he should watch from. He duly obliged and walked off without looking back. He was too interested in searching out the bookmaker from earlier.

She walked the same stairs down towards the steel cage, ringed with barbed wire, followed by the large man. To the crowd, his role was to stop a fighter having second thoughts and fleeing, but to her, he was an invisible irrelevance. She was too focused and she was not for fleeing.

The crowd saw her tall, determined figure approaching the ring and some started shouting sexist abuse while others gestured their disapproval. No one had expected a woman in this vicious arena. Some started to throw objects, both in her direction and towards the ring, but Shoshanna walked forward, unfazed and uncaring, for she had a greater task ahead of her. They didn't know her. They didn't know what she was capable of. They didn't know what she had done in her past and they certainly didn't know what she planned to do in front of them. If they had known, they might have been more respectful.

The male-dominated testosterone-filled crowd did not expect to see a woman fight their champion, but Bohdan had done a good job. He had paid a lot of money to arrange the match and was gambling on his limited knowledge of Shoshanna's past to get much more back.

Likewise, her pending adversary didn't know whom he was fighting, nor that it was to be a woman.

Vitschencko stood in the ring talking to another man. He had his back to her when the cage door opened. The noise of the gate opening and then being locked again did not distract him. His arrogance and confidence meant he did not need to determine the size, and strength of his opponent. His attitude was such that he believed he had no opponents worthy of him.

When Vitschencko's colleague saw her, however, he whispered into the fighter's ear. Very slowly and without swivelling his massive body around, he turned his head to look at her.

He was a beast of a man. Standing six foot four tall, and weighing over one hundred and twenty kilograms. He had kept himself in good shape since his forced departure from the Russian special forces, Spetsnaz. He had scars across his chest, which he would claim were from fighting opponents with knives when he was unarmed, just to make it a fair fight. His thirst for killing had moved from gun to hand and he was good at it.

He turned to face her and, stepping a little closer towards her, he thrust his chest out in an intimidating manner. A smile spread across his lips. The crowd may not have wanted a woman in the ring, but he had no issues fighting one.

Shoshanna looked him in the eye. Did he recognise her?

No, she sensed he did not see her as someone he once fought alongside. He only saw his next victim. She saw hatred and revulsion, as she did that day many years earlier with the murder of so many children in the inferno.

Bohdan had adopted a vantage point near what he assumed was an exit, but not before he had placed a very hefty bet on Shoshanna to win. He had received both massive odds and laughter.

"Hey, bitch, are you lost?" Vitschencko said, walking right up to her. "Are you looking for the supermarket?" he taunted, chuckling with mirth at his own joke. Turning to face his charged-up audience, he gestured to them. Holding his hands in a cupping manner over his chest to imitate Shoshanna's breasts, he shouted, "Do you see them? Do you want to see them? I will rip her top off first, then I will rip her face off. Get your money out!"

Vitschencko's sidekick left the ring as instructed and then, as the cage door was being shut, Shoshanna walked up to the referee and in a lightning-quick second, kicked him between the legs before slamming the side of his head with an open hand. Down he fell, like a log, out cold. She pointed to the two men who seemed to be in charge outside the cage. *Will he recognise my voice?* she thought. *Too late now, anyway.*

"You, get this low life out of my ring. We don't need a ref." Then, turning to face her opponent, she spoke again, "You think we need a ref? You feel safer with one?"

Vitschencko smiled at her. He hadn't recognised her and had been a little taken back by her assault on the referee.

The dazed man was quickly taken away and, as he was placed on a nearby chair, the door of the cage closed once again. Now there were only two inside.

She decided to start the fight. Why would she wait?

"Hey, ugly man, are we doing this or not?" she asked. "Do you want to see what's in my shopping bag or are you as cowardly as you are repulsive?"

She continued, "Now remember, ugly man, make it very clear when you are submitting. I might not hear above the noise of these scum." As she was considering more words, he lunged at her.

So it started.

His first swing of a clenched fist missed, but the fight had begun, and so did the loud and raucous shouts from those outside the cage.

Again, he lunged forward, both arms swinging around in front of him, but again, they were easily avoided by Shoshanna. He did not yet take her seriously, so his approach was careless. His attacks were easily evaded for now.

"Hey, ugly man, have you done this before?" she goaded Vitschencko.

She would find out the answer soon enough.

When he did catch her and stop her dancing around the makeshift ring, he would make her suffer. It would only be a matter of time.

The crowd bade for blood. Bohdan watched, more and more apprehensive, while the two protagonists danced away. One would be fleet-footed, and duck and block, while the other rampaged forwards, seeking the right angle to trap his foe.

Then, contact. The crowd erupted. Shoshanna stumbled back a little and Bohdan clenched both hands into fists. He was now expecting the worst.

The strength of his blow had powered through her block and with almost full energy, had landed on the side of her temple. Shoshanna staggered back and, dazed, fell to the dust. Immediately, her survival instinct took over and she rose back to her feet, raising her guard. She knew never to be stranded and injured on the ground.

Vitschencko had decided not to follow up on the downed Shoshanna but instead, stood, hands on his wide hips, smiling at her. She had been lucky this time.

Had he followed up, he would surely have inflicted real injury. His arrogant, sexist attitude had unexpectedly saved her this time. When she decided to fight back and he recognised her as a true opponent, then his leniency would likely stop.

"I see you have very little in your shopping bag, bitch," he bellowed, more to the audience than to his victim.

Rubbing her head, she again squared up to him. "We'll see, ugly man. Are you ready or do you need a rest?"

Addressing the crowd, Vitschencko shouted, "Bet more, I will down this bitch when I choose to. But for now, I have fun, so bet more!"

The noise level increased another notch as those who were not already laughing and shouting joined in the cacophony. A flurry of hands clasping banknotes shot into the air and the runners were again busy collecting the cash.

Bohdan gripped the edge of his seat nervously. He stared at her, searching for a sign that this was part of her plan. He couldn't see one. He wondered about his huge wager on the outcome. His apprehension was about to ramp up.

"So, as I said, ugly man, do you need a rest?" she said again sarcastically.

"Bitch, I do you when I am ready," he sneered, still encouraging the crowd to shout louder and bet more money on him.

Ominously, he stopped rallying spectators after a few seconds and turned towards her. "Now I am ready, bitch," and with the words still ringing out, he again lunged at her. He made contact immediately with a fist to her shoulder, after she managed to part-block it, steering it from her face. A second hand came rapidly after the first punch and simply pushed her violently backwards, hitting her just above her left breast.

The crowd, already standing, now started jumping and bumping into each other. They anticipated a quick end and a further profitable pay out, courtesy of their reigning champion.

Shoshanna fell badly into the barbed wire, again dazed, but this time her clothing got tangled, and a few cuts started to weep blood across her arms and the back of her neck.

Bohdan stood and held his head in his hands. Calculating his massive loss, he willed her to get up quickly.

This time, Vitschencko walked forward towards her. He towered over the fallen Shoshanna and looked down at her. "You're going hungry tonight, bitch. Nothing in your shopping bag…" And he landed a heavy boot into her lower back, striking her kidney hard, punctuating his verbal abuse.

Shoshanna let out a cry of pain and fell further into the barbed wire, cutting her shoulder and cheek. The crowd cheered more, some shouting abuse at her. Bohdan considered leaving, much money lost, but just as he was contemplating it, he saw something that instinctively made him sit back down.

The anguish had left her face and as she fixed her stare on Bohdan, she smiled. To the crowd's surprise, she winked as she began ripping her top off to free herself from the wire. Blood dripped out of a number of heavy scratch wounds all over her upper body, but for Shoshanna, this was par for the course. It was neither a surprise, nor a distraction.

Luckily for her, Vitschencko had again decided to strut around the cage, taking in his plaudits instead of finishing her off. His arrogance was to be his downfall. He stopped when he saw her rise to her feet, minus her top, exposing her bra and rock-hard abdominal muscles to the raucous crowd.

"You see, I told you I would get the bitch's top off! Vitschencko never fails his fans!" he shouted, whilst beating his chest triumphantly.

Shoshanna put a hand to her cheek to determine the extent of the cut there. Looking down at her hand, she saw her blood, but it didn't bother her any.

"Time to stop this game, ugly man. Now I am really pissed off with you and I don't care for these animals looking at my breasts," she said angrily to his face.

This time, she started the proceedings.

She moved quickly towards him, raising her fist as if to swing. Vitschencko stretched both arms out, hands open in anticipation of the strike. However, it didn't come.

Instead, knowing she had to get her huge opponent off balance to level the field, she ducked under and inside his defensive guard. At the same time as she lunged forward, she used her boot to crack into, then down his left shin. Her left arm rose up and into his groin before she rolled fast out from underneath, ending up behind him.

The speed and accuracy of the blows had him, momentarily, crippled and bent in half. She knew this would not last long. Disable or be disabled – she had to press her furious attack.

Stepping slightly forward, she landed the toe of her boot in her opponent's face; Vitschencko's nose seemed to explode. The force of the kick lifted his head upwards, just as she expected it would. Blood from his nose flew into the air. She followed with two open-hand slaps hard across his closest ear, further extending his moment of disorientation.

She was too busy to notice, but the crowd had quieted with disbelief at what they were witnessing.

Shoshanna forced a boot hard into the back of Vitschencko's right leg, further weakening his centre of gravity. Her elbow then fell hard down onto the back of his head, and a second time and a third, before the giant man fell to the ground, completely addled and bloodied. It had happened so quickly that he had no time to recover. Her military hand-to-hand training, that had saved her life in war so many times, was working for her again.

Taking advantage of his momentum, downward towards the dust, she shoved one knee on his neck while the rest of her body weight pushed on his back.

She wasn't finished yet.

Grabbing his hand away from his nose, which he had instinctively put there to protect it, she went about forcing each finger as far back against the joint as she was able, confident that each time, they would dislocate or break. He was now unable to utilise his superior strength and pull her down. Then, moving her knee from the back of his neck, she landed two firm hits to the face, as close to his shattered nose as she could manage.

Certain he would struggle to get to his feet, she lifted herself up and towered above him.

"This is for my cut face," she said, thundering down the sole of her boot onto his exposed and bloodied nose.

"This is for fighting a woman, you coward," she said almost calmly, despite the physical effort being exerted, as a second boot slammed down into his kidneys. Then, with a third heavy attack, she leered towards him and spat out, "And this is for ripping my shirt," as she launched, knees-first, onto his head.

Vitschencko lay in the dirt, bloodied and broken. His breathing was erratic due to his multiple injuries and the dust he was inhaling through his mouth.

Now in an overwhelming position of strength, Shoshanna slipped one hand under his head and the other gripped his chin. For a fleeting second, she turned her head and looked out of the cage. She now saw the crowd, bewildered and strangely quiet. Without further delay she readied herself.

"Oh, Vitschencko, I never liked you in Syria and I hate you more now. Before you die, remember the children you burned alive. I do. Every day," she leant towards him, menacingly shadowing his bloodied body.

As her grip tightened on his face, she noticed him staring wildly at her through his right eye. It widened for a second as best as it could through the blood and the bruising. He finally recognised her from those years back when they had conducted an operation together. His eye focused on her as he tried to speak. Then, as quickly as it had opened, it shut for good. She sharply and forcefully twisted his head round as far as she was able, and upon hearing his neck break, released her grip and pulled herself to her feet.

She stood for a moment, looking down at the motionless body slumped in a mess at her feet. She then turned towards the cage door and opened it herself, the previously on-hand helpers struck dumb with shock, before stepping out. She grabbed the dirty towel still lying across a chair and wiped her hands clean of Vitschencko's blood.

Bohdan had rushed down to meet her, after first collecting a bag full of money from the disbelieving Chinese bookie.

"Best we go now; now, Agnon, before it turns nasty. You were not supposed to kill him – they no longer have a champion to bet on," he said in a rushed and slightly panicked voice.

She stood for a moment, defiant against the crowd.

"Your jacket, take it off."

Bohdan did as asked and after covering herself up, Shoshanna followed him out of the immediate arena.

When the door slammed behind them and they were again back in the first corridor, Bohdan began to run towards the outside exit.

"Quick, before they come after us," he shouted, now several yards in front of her.

Shoshanna agreed with his assumption and likewise began to run. Bohdan forced the exit open, and ran out into the daylight and heat. The dust flew up into the air around them as their feet pounded down. She followed very closely behind him as they quickly made their way to his jeep.

"So I still need you then, it seems," she said as he started the engine and put it into gear. "To the railway station, Bohdan; then you can rid yourself of me for good. We will be even." She half smiled as the car raced away, leaving dust and stones spraying around.

As they pulled away from the warehouse, Bohdan could see several men gathering outside in his rear-view mirror. He had been right to leave as quickly as they had done and now he just had a couple of hours more with Agnon before he could begin to count exactly how much money he had made from the fight.

Both were quiet during the drive.

Shoshanna sat back into the seat, now a little more uncomfortable from her injuries and thought about her vengeance for the children in the burning building. She hoped the nightmares would leave her now, but wasn't confident she could ever forget. She also started to ponder her next target. This had not yet ended for her. Both she and the world needed further retribution from those special operators who had killed at will, and walked away, only now to profit from death. She spent many a night convinced of duty, of the need for the soldier and the special forces operator, but was still convinced that some were not worthy to be classed as such.

She thought about Jegertroppen, or Hunter Force, but especially she thought about Helene Marte. Helene would be her next target, but for now, Shoshanna mostly thought about the avenging of the children and her injuries, which would need rest.

The journey to the station was thankfully uneventful. Neither spoke much to the other.

Soon enough, Bohdan pulled up at the station and the sudden stop jolted Shoshanna. She had slept a bit and he had simply driven. He had not betrayed her but had done as they had agreed. This growing trust in him was not missed by either of them.

"You can keep the jacket, Agnon," he said, holding a hand out in front of him.

She duly took his hand, something that would not have happened a short while earlier that day.

"Bohdan, I still don't like you," she said with a smile. "You will never amount to anything, you waste of space." And with that, Shoshanna opened the door and got out. She had no possessions other than a small rucksack, which she now carried in one hand.

"You need some money?" he shouted after her. And for a few seconds, she smiled at his kindness.

"No, just make sure you invest it well." And as she turned to walk towards the ticket office, she stopped again. This caught his eye.

"Bohdan, thank you for helping me end it with Vitschencko," she said, nodding to him before turning and walking into the railway station, knowing she would not see her new friend ever again.

Bohdan started the engine and drove off.

They would not meet again, but they left each other surprisingly content and appreciative. Shoshanna bought her ticket and sat down in the waiting room. The next train was not for over an hour. It was time for more sleep. Her damaged body needed rest.

Chapter 6
London

It was raining hard that day in London.

Shoshanna couldn't remember a time when it didn't rain hard in London.

Today, as she stood on the rooftop of her flat, with only a long t-shirt covering her, the rain felt particularly heavy. Soaked through, the shape of her athletic body left nothing to the imagination. The clothing clung tight to her, revealing the curves and tone of her finely tuned physique. Her nipples were erect and showing, with her long hair, running down her back, acting as a route for the water to reach the ground. As she looked up into the falling rain high above her, feeling each and every drop impact upon her face, she felt temporarily free. Invigorated. She felt almost cleansed, as if the rain could magically wash her past from her mind, leaving images of happier times back in Israel with her mother in their garden.

She knew that he was most likely watching her from behind a curtain in his room. Shoshanna had an admirer a distance away, across the gap between the two buildings. She had already spotted him on several occasions when she had gone out onto the roof to take a break from the monotony of her featureless room and the wait for the right timing of her next assignment.

He was perhaps early teens and clearly shy, but the shape of her almost naked body this morning had drawn him out from behind the sanctuary of his bedroom curtain. He stood and watched her, his mouth slightly open. She turned and faced him. He would have to imagine the detail of her body this time, for it was difficult to see clearly in the heavy rain. No doubt as she walked back towards the window entry into her flat and out of sight, he would do just that in the privacy of his room. Imagine.

"No need for a shower then, Sho," she said out loud as she walked the wooden floorboards into the bathroom, leaving a trail of rain water behind her. Throwing her soaked t-shirt in the bath, she grabbed a towel and began to rub her naked body dry.

For a moment, she stopped and eyed the tattoo on her right thigh, now slightly disfigured due to the recent injury incurred during the fight with Vitschencko. She had a tiny, fresh scar running across the image of a winged angel descending down to earth. The scar, running vertically through the design, seemed to show the angel split between original purity and hope, and a twisted and vulgar creature. The cut from the fight seemed to rip its upper body and face in two.

"Now I seem to have two angels to follow," she said, again, out loud to herself. "Which one am I to be, the good or the evil?"

With a slight lip movement upward, she acknowledged that she already knew which one it was.

She tied her hair up, slung on figure-hiding clothing and headed out into the morning rain. It wasn't as heavy, but it was still spitting slightly on her face as she walked the streets towards the coffee house and the pre-arranged meeting with her only worldly friend. The streets of London were crowded, as they always were. She revelled in the anonymity afforded by the busy pavements, walking through the unsuspecting public without fear of a tap on her shoulder, or worse, not feeling anything at all as an assassin's bullet ended her life.

A short bus ride later, having sat amongst the prams and pensioners en route to the shops, she hopped off a short way from the designated café.

Shoshanna stood for a few minutes in a doorway across from the coffee shop and watched her long-time friend, Lisa, with a trained eye monitoring the street movement at the same time. A few years back, Shoshanna had first met Lisa in a similar coffee shop. Lisa had 'come to her rescue' when a chancer tried to steal her phone, carelessly left visible on the table. Holding the door shut and not allowing the thief's escape, Shoshanna regained her property, and the thief gained a highly visible and sore black bruise around one eye. The two women had later laughed about the incident and exchanged numbers. They had met again since that day, but today and on this occasion, Shoshanna felt anxious about meeting her only real friend.

Then, take-away coffee in hand, she allowed herself to drift off to a different place. She felt the warmth of the coffee and it was strangely reassuring. She went back to the parade ground and the hours spent in training, those few years back. How she longed for those simple and structured days to return. She wondered how she went from brilliant soldier to renegade warrior and how it had not taken her long to get there. Her mind, and her body were now much different from the positive and assertive soldier back in Israel.

Then, as quickly as she drifted away, she was back. She was back on the streets of London, across from the rendezvous point with her only friend.

When she was confident that what she saw was routine, with no imminent surprises, she crossed the road towards her friend and went into the café. Each and every pedestrian she passed was totally unaware that they shared space with a trained killer – one who could end life with her bare hands. Instead, most looked down at their phones, or just walked along, blissfully unaware.

"Sorry for being late, Lisa," she said as she approached her table. "The traffic was so bad that even the bus lanes are clogged."

"Hey, you, no worries, I am just glad you made it. You're wet. Don't you own an umbrella, Sho? It's not like living in the Med here, you know?" came the reply from her close friend, who had now stood and was hugging Shoshanna, not really expecting an answer to her question about umbrellas.

"Anyway, is that cold?" Shoshanna pointed to the mug. "Do you want a fresh coffee?"

"Shall we go somewhere better, where we can have a vino or two, missy?" Lisa replied. She hadn't seen her friend for such a long time and felt giddy with the thought of an hour or two of conversation.

"I'd rather not, if you don't mind. I've checked this place and it's safe," replied Shoshanna. Lisa thought it was a bit out of character and a puzzled look crossed her face. Shoshanna tried to ignore it.

"Ok, fine. Mine's a latte please, up you go, girl."

Shoshanna went to the counter, and stood and waited her turn to be served, before returning to the table a few minutes later, two lattes and two slices of chocolate cake in hand.

"Yum, chocolate. So, stranger, what have you been up to recently? And I want to know everything," Lisa asked, settling into her seat as the two then relaxed back and began their long overdue catch up. Shoshanna wished that she could tell someone the truth, but as good a friend as Lisa was, the truth was pretty shocking for anyone and probably unbelievable. She smiled as she imagined telling her she'd just killed a Russian psychopath in a hand-to-hand cage fight.

"Oh, you know, killing time and stuff," Shoshanna replied, quelling the urge to blurt out the truth. "No, well, really, I have just been travelling around trying to get inspiration for that travel book that I have been trying to write for years."

"Great, Sho, and where are we with the writing?" Lisa asked with a glint in her eye. She already knew the answer, however. When she had last seen Shoshanna, around twelve months earlier, she had found excuses not to start the book and Lisa expected it to be the same.

Shoshanna had bailed on numerous meetings with Lisa. She had met her several years earlier, cold and wet on a London street, after a surveillance operation had gone badly wrong and she had to leave the scene rapidly, unable to make her way to the safe house.

Instead, this friend in front of her had taken her in that night and given her shelter, believing her to be a cash-strapped student who was travelling the world trying to find inspiration for a book.

"Well, you know me, why write today when you can put it off for an adventure somewhere else tomorrow?" Shoshanna answered, this time not facing her friend but instead sipping on her coffee and looking around the shop.

The two talked for a while longer about Lisa's work in radio and how she juggled it with two rather lively toddlers to bring up on her own after her husband left her for another woman years earlier. She had found adult company in women only, thereafter, and this blossomed fully towards her mysterious travelling friend, Shoshanna, each and every time she was in London.

Shoshanna then reciprocated with fictitious cover stories of fun travel from around the world, keeping her closest, perhaps, only real friend, in the dark about her violent activities.

Shoshanna felt guilty about misleading Lisa. Part of her was desperate to open up and just tell someone, enjoying the release of pressure that it may allow. But she instantly suppressed these feelings and reverted back to limning images and pictures of her travel with words.

First, it would be the beautiful island of Santorini, and then she would counter this with a horrid experience on the other side of the world, and in doing so, she kept her cover story lifelike and believable. She would describe the sun setting on the island caldera, turning the sea orange and flame-like. Then, she would tell her friend of the hellhole accommodation and the drug-dealing streets of Venezuela. The good with the bad kept the lie more real. Shoshanna was actually well travelled, but instead of beaches and cocktails, her journeys tended to include looking down the barrel of a gun and ending life.

Nearly ninety minutes had passed, and the two had consumed another coffee each and a selection of cakes. Shoshanna knew that she would soon have to leave her friend but was reluctant to break this spell. Sitting there with Lisa, she could almost believe her own illusion that she had a normal life. Lisa had a life, a proper life and would likely want to get back to that soon. She had left the children with her elderly mother, and would need to get them home and fed soon enough. Shoshanna suspected this, but for now, she wanted the chat and the friendly company to continue for as long as it could, she was tentatively wondering about suggesting a third coffee when the decision was abruptly taken away from her. They were interrupted.

"Can I detect the tones of a Hebrew accent, someone from Israel, here in South-East London?"

The voice startled Shoshanna a little, but instantly, she regained her composure and calmed her heart. She could see the reflection of a young man standing behind her in the window next to Lisa and determined that he was no threat.

"No, you're mistaken, it's Scottish, you fool," she replied to the stranger, without looking around. Lisa gave the man a hard stare and he knew that he was not welcome at their table.

He turned, take-away coffee in hand and left the shop, mumbling to himself.

"Perhaps, we can walk and talk, Sho. No more rude interruptions?" said Lisa. "You know, I don't get your accent. Is it recognisable then, like Israeli? I just hear you…"

Shoshanna didn't answer. She knew she stood out in that respect and in doing so, she was recognisable – that was a bad thing.

The interruption had turned out to be a blessing in disguise for Shoshanna. She had not wanted to go back to her cold, dull flat alone and wait. She was actually relaxing around her friend, a type of relaxation that she had not felt in a very long time.

"That said, Sho, my offer is conditional," Lisa hinted as she stood and put on her coat. "It's wine time, my friend, and I know where we are going. Come on, let's go." Lisa had picked up her bag, which Shoshanna noticed had baby wipes inside and, smiling at the contrast between the nature of her own work versus that of her friend bringing up two children on her own, she did as instructed and followed Lisa promptly out of the shop.

They walked for a while through the streets, crossing roads occasionally, neither saying much over the noise of the lorries and cars that clogged London's streets, until they arrived at an obscure and slightly hidden doorway between two fast-food shops. Lisa stopped and turned to her friend.

"Ready?" she asked, with a cheeky smile.

"Ready? For what?" said Shoshanna, staring blankly at the unassuming doorway.

"This," and Lisa opened the door, revealing a long dark stairway down into a partly illuminated basement room. The stairway had a string of glittering stars down as if to show first-time entrants where to go.

The friends walked down the stairs, with Lisa first and Shoshanna close behind, becoming a little bit anxious. This uncertainty was not something she was used to or initially liked. She much preferred planning every minute of every hour of her violent existence. It was a method of existence that seemed to keep her alive, but now, she was in the hands of another, one she trusted, but another all the same.

They reached the bottom and turned a corner and were faced with a glowing sign, the source of the slight illumination seen from the stairway.

The sign read 'Below the Smoke'.

"Relax, Sho, it's a bar," said Lisa as she pushed on the door below the sign and entered. As the light and air from inside started to creep out towards them, so did the overwhelming noise of music and laughter.

Shoshanna followed Lisa into the bar, staying close to her friend. She was more relaxed now, feeling strangely at ease when she held her friend's hand as they walked through the suited men towards the bar.

It seemed to Shoshanna that the only other females in the place were all behind the bar serving cocktails to groups of men, smartly dressed but acting loud and obnoxious.

"It's a men-only bar. I think some private club for finance tossers," Lisa shouted over the noise. "Let's get a drink quickly and then the bouncer won't kick us out."

"No, I have a better idea," replied Shoshanna, as she took her jacket off revealing a tight, short t-shirt. She was more relaxed, here and now, than at any time in recent memory. The adventure of doing normal fun things with a girlfriend was making her so happy and chilled that she was game for anything this day would bring her.

Shoshanna walked into the middle of a group of five loud, drunk men and spoke, "Right, you lot, we're not allowed in here as we are the superior sex and this place only lets rats in. So, to stop us being thrown out, which one of you is going to buy my friend and me a drink?"

Then, as if rehearsed, all five men grabbed their wallets in unison and thrust them into the air as if holding Excalibur.

"You see, my lovely Lisa, this is how I survive on my trips abroad," said Shoshanna with the biggest grin Lisa had ever seen. This made Lisa smile, and, like her friend, she made herself more comfortable and noticeable by removing her own jacket, and throwing it into the arms of the closest alcohol benefactor.

"You can buy me a Prosecco," Lisa purred.

"They don't sell that shit here, doll," came the reply. "Best we share another bottle of Bollie!" Lisa's chosen sponsor turned and gestured to a scantily dressed barmaid. Sure enough, another bottle of expensive Champagne followed quickly after the order of two men vying for the sole attention of Shoshanna.

Shoshanna grabbed the arms of the two remaining men, and the newly assembled party walked from the bar and sat together in a private booth, leaving the two original party members, who'd bought her a drink, to wonder what had just happened.

Men would walk by this noisy group and wonder what two beautiful women were doing in their private, men-only club. None of them complained, however, but instead, threw envious glances towards the three men sitting with them.

The bouncers would occasionally walk by, and try to find the right opportunity to do their jobs and rid the club of the two female intruders. However, each time they approached, they would receive a handshake loaded with a few bank notes to encourage them to look elsewhere.

An hour had passed since they sat down and by now, all five were beginning to feel the effects of too much Champagne. The two men Shoshanna brought with her to the booth tried to outdo the other for her affections and both had lost many times over. Shoshanna had her eye on someone else. She was enjoying the time and the relaxation, but around men, there was always something that stopped her from fully opening up and being her real self. Her male-dominated and often violent past had darkened her impression of men forever. Instead, Shoshanna felt warmth from her female friend sitting close to her, who, on occasions, would look her directly in the eyes and smile.

Lisa had her arm around her temporary escort, but she too felt like something was not right with the configuration of the group. The alcohol was running dry again on the table and while both women had no doubt they could magically conjure up more from the wallets of one of their 'friends' at the table, almost instantaneously both women rose to their feet, grabbed their few possessions and prepared to leave.

"Hey, where are you going, ladies? We are just getting started here," said one man.

"Shut up, Charles," said another. "These birds go to the loos together to discuss strategy and, personally, mate, I think they want to discuss how to bomb you out, you ugly fuck." Charles raised a middle finger out towards his loudmouth friend and smiled.

"Don't be long, ladies, the action's all here," said Charles, still believing that they were actually going to the toilets. Shoshanna left the booth first and, glancing behind her to see Lisa there, walked forward towards the noise and the crowd of the other financers in the men-only club.

"They're not coming back, you know," said the third man, who seemed the soberest, as he watched Shoshanna grab the hand of Lisa, and walk past the bar and out of sight. "The loos are behind us, so why do you think they have walked that way, then?" he continued, now with a smug look on his face. He had sensed that they were being used by the two women, but he had no real issue with continuing to pay for drinks while they stayed and laughed with them.

"Bitches!" shouted the second man, now realising he was a few hundred pounds down on the deal, with no foreplay or even a phone number left to look forward to.

"Right," remarked Charles as he stood up. "I don't know about you two, but I'm right up for it now and we aren't going to get laid in this place. Who's coming to a proper fuckin' mixed club, then?"

With that, the three friends stood and, grabbing their jackets, headed out towards the exit of the club. Although none of them mentioned it, silently all three secretly admired the two women and how they had taken them for fools.

Meanwhile, with a spring in their step, Lisa and Shoshanna headed out along the street towards the Underground. Shoshanna's bed and breakfast was only a couple of stops away, and both women knew exactly what that meant.

Lisa texted her babysitting mother, letting her know she would be late home and that she should not wait up for her. Shoshanna had no one to inform, but like Lisa, expected to be up late that night. For the men left behind in the bar, drunk, bewildered and belligerent, they would have no idea that Lisa and Shoshanna only had eyes for each other.

Chapter 7
Nightmare

Lisa tried to wake her but Shoshanna was too far gone into her murky past to awaken properly. Something was reoccurring in Shoshanna's mind and while Lisa felt guilty leaving her to it, she also suspected that this night-time event she was witnessing, was a regular occurrence and so left the room to try to get sleep in the spare room.

Shoshanna tossed and turned for a while longer. Occasionally, she would call out, waking Lisa now sleeping in the room next door. Her noises were confusing and as she listened, Lisa tried and failed to figure out what was happening in the mind of her friend. She seemed to be recalling some violent act or acts in her nightmare.

If she had stayed with her friend in the bed, she may have seen Shoshanna clench and unclench her fists as they seemed to be holding on to some imaginary item, her index finger moving rapidly and independently of her other fingers as if firing a gun. She would also have seen her sit upright in a sudden violent motion, and her eyes open as Shoshanna looked and felt at her chest, although still not awake but remaining in her unconscious state and nightmare place.

Then, as sudden as she sprang up and checked her body over for injuries, Shoshanna lay back down, the fire in her eyes eased and then closed, and her breathing returned to a more normal rhythmical form. She had accepted what was happening in her head and not fighting it, and as a result, she could sleep again while the demons of her past played their merry tricks in her conscience.

"Operation, we are compromised. I repeat, we have been compromised."

"Operation, repeat and confirm."

"Operation, I repeat we have been compromised, they are everywhere, request immediate evac."

Shoshanna seemed to move her head away from her imaginary noise and gun fire.

Operation – evac request confirmed.

"Please, urgent evac, they are everywhere. We are surrounded and low on ammo, please hurry, Operation."

Operation – "confirmed, return fire and move to a green zone, air support is up and en route to you."

Operation – "we have your co-ordinates, air support is up and en route to you. Return fire and await further instructions."

"They are everywhere, operation, they are in the building, no time for evac, ammo is low. Capture by these bastards is not an option."

Operation – "return your team to safe line. Evac is minutes away, I repeat, evac is minutes away."

"They are too close for evac. I request air strike on my coordinates. We cannot be captured by these bastards. Repeat, request immediate air strike on my coordinates."

Operation – "negative, help is imminent, go to green zone and return fire."

"Call in the bloody air strike and do it now. Let's take these bastards with us. We cannot be captured and paraded by these bastards. Do it now!"

Operation – "Please confirm request."

"Now, air strike now, confirmed."

Shoshanna was living the final moments of her team once again. She would do so many times in the future as she had done in the past. She would feel her guilt for the rest of her days every time she managed to get sleep.

When she woke several days later, Shoshanna found herself in a makeshift hospital with what she believed was a Kurdish uniformed guard standing by her bed. Her body ached and she was in excruciating pain. There was a drip entering a vein in her arm and another, red in colour protruding from a wound on her abdomen.

She was confused, bewildered, and falling in and out of consciousness, however, she seemed to have survived the air strike. It was the only explanation. The Islamic Spear would certainly not have taken her injured to hospital. Instead, they would have dragged her through the streets until she died.

It was the only explanation. She had survived the air strike and these people, these Kurds had taken her from the rubble and brought her here.

What of the others, she thought, yet, as she tried to speak and ask, she felt too much pain in her throat.

Chapter 8
Dragon

This would be her hardest target yet.

The British destroyer, *Dragon,* was a formidable machine. The vessel had a displacement of nine thousand four hundred tonnes of water. She was powered by two huge Rolls Royce gas turbine engines. And then, there was her weapons capability.

The ship was replete with an awesome array of air surveillance and tracking radar systems. This was her self-defence capacity. Her attack potential was much more awesome.

HMS *Dragon* was rammed full of Sea Viper missiles and at four thousand kilometres per hour, they were the fastest moving thing on the planet. The extra Aster missiles, Harpoon launchers, thirty-millimetre Gatling guns and general-purpose machine guns were likewise formidable. Lastly, *Dragon* housed an attack Lynx Wildcat helicopter capable of hunting down and destroying those that were stupid enough to take her on, be they smugglers, military force or individual.

Indeed, this was going to be Shoshanna's hardest target yet.

Shoshanna was not, however, taking on the whole ship. Her aim was to make a stealthy incursion on board, evading the human security, then track down one specific crew member, followed by their elimination and then escape. It would be that simplistic.

Her mobile received a text message. Standing on the back of the Thames Clipper en route upstream towards Greenwich, she looked down at the message.

'Hey, you. Sneaking off without saying goodbye… typical. Don't be long back this time. Lisa x.'

As soon as she read the message, she deleted it, deleting the number in a further few seconds. The contact details of her only friend in this world were now gone. She couldn't risk her friend being caught up in her troubles. Anyway, a part of her knew she would never see Lisa again. The same part of her that knew she would be caught out one time and it would all end badly.

She stood alone at the back of the Clipper as the engines powered up, and it sped forward towards the home of time, Greenwich and her next contact.

Shoshanna watched the multitude of former warehouses and wharfs, now plush residences, go past until the announcement came over the boat's tannoy.

'Next stop is Greenwich. Please make your way to the front of the boat to alight.'

She walked up the ramp and onto the jetty, hidden amongst dozens of tourists and visitors, to one of London's most beautiful locations – Greenwich, the centre of all things maritime and historical that mattered. The home of the meridian line, which determines time around the rest of the world and where, moored a few dozen yards off shore, HMS *Dragon* lay in wait for her.

It certainly was a beast of a vessel. Shapley, impressive, silent and deadly. But so was Shoshanna. It would be a hard kill, but it would be a rewarding and challenging one also. She stood at the top of the ramp, and for a fleeting moment, lost herself in the sights and sounds of the Thames and the tourists.

"Move along, please." She was woken from her thoughts, realising that she was blocking the exit and causing a slight build-up of eager tourists.

"Yes, of course, sorry," she said as she stepped aside and considered her next move.

As she walked off towards the town centre, she noticed a group of sailors on what she assumed was shore leave. With her target boat the only navy vessel currently on the river, she decided to follow them, and eavesdrop on their conversations and plans. Perhaps, they could tell her something useful. Predictably, they entered a nearby pub and headed towards the bar.

"Hey, who's going to buy a girl a drink?" she said suggestively.

The three men turned around to the voice. They saw a flirtatious, tanned and athletic woman smiling at them. Shoshanna's dry run with the city financers the night before had got her in the mood to carry on with this approach. Again, it would work. Being ship-bound for six months at a time would leave these three targets easy prey for any beautiful woman.

Without waiting for a response, Shoshanna walked into their small group and lodged herself on the shoulder of the closest sailor.

"Gin and slimline tonic, honey," she said, staring right at him and smiling.

"Em, well, gin it is then," he said, rather embarrassed. "Lads, seems it's my round, so what you having?"

With the drinks pending, Shoshanna took her new navy friend by the arm and walked him firmly but closely to a nearby table. They both sat.

"Lads, bring our drinks over, but you don't have to join us," he said to his two bemused friends at the bar. "The cash is on the bar."

"No, wait, you have to join us," Shoshanna barked back. "No one said I was a one-man girl."

Her seated companion looked disappointed but taken aback at the same time and now his two smiling friends were walking towards their table with the drinks.

"So then, boys," she started, not wasting time, intent on directing her acquired sailors towards the matter at hand – perhaps, not what they were hoping to get out of the conversation.

"How long are you lovely boys here in Greenwich? I assume from your smartly pressed uniforms, you are sailors from that big boat on the river?"

"Yes," started one, but he was quickly interrupted by another.

"I speak here, lads; I'm senior rank," came the formal reply from the third man.

Shoshanna had already established the group's leader and commanding rank by the markings on his uniform. He would, perhaps, be the one with most information about her real on-board target.

"Oh yes, you are," she said with a teasing smile. "You have a strip on your shoulders and your friends don't."

"So, tell me, Commander, you are a commander or captain or something, aren't you? How long are you here in my home town and are you allowed to enjoy yourself when you have shore leave?"

They could not believe their apparent luck, and as their guard lowered and the alcohol flowed, they opened up to her.

The next hour went past very slowly for Shoshanna, and no doubt, very quickly for the three sailors sitting and laughing with the often-tactile woman sitting next to them. When it did end and she stood, having taken the phone number of one, thanked them for the drinks and walked quickly out of the pub, she deposited the scribbled number in an ash tray on the bar near the exit.

She had what she needed. She knew the ship was to leave for open seas in forty-eight hours, so her plan had to accelerate.

It had been a valuable hour – especially when they started to talk about their VIP temporary guests. One of these guests would get a visit from Shoshanna within forty-eight hours. For now, however, it was back to her bed and some food, before reviewing her plan.

Sitting alone in her room, Shoshanna closed her eyes and allowed herself to relax and reflect. Lying down on the bed, she could feel the air from the open window blow gently over her body. It was cooling on the outside but had no effect on the burning heat within her soul.

The Jegertroppen, or Hunter Force, had a special place in her plan. They remained the world's only all-female special forces unit and she had come across them a few years back when she was temporarily stationed in Norway.

Her Shayetet 13 unit had been assigned a training role with the then new Hunter Force and as Shoshanna was the first female graduate in her troop, it was felt that she should lead the small training team.

She remembered being hugely impressed with their physical power and technical ability, but she remembered more that she had been impressed with their commander, Helene Marte.

Standing taller than Shoshanna, who was no insignificant figure herself, Marte was an impressive woman. Shoshanna had instant respect for this officer who, when in full operational uniform, would not stand out from the male operators and indeed often surprised other soldiers when she would reveal herself as female at the de-brief.

The two had started a sort of friendship those years back, but now this would end.

Shoshanna had no need for friends.

More than this, she was driven to end the special forces world from exploiting its notoriety for personal financial gain, a greedy world her former friend was now blowing wide open. The realm of the secret operator was exactly that, secret and together with Marte amassing huge sums of money from her regular TV appearances, she also had a past that only Shoshanna knew.

The night before her training unit was to return to Israel, Helene Marte and Shoshanna went off the base, and into the small town of Hammerfest, in the north of the country, where the locals all knew who they were but kept their secret out of a sense of duty and pride.

They would share select private stories and operational matters.

It was their way of off-loading some of the emotional tension that builds inside the minds of all operators. On this night, however, Helene Marte was to sign her death warrant. She did not know this yet and neither did Shoshanna when she listened to her comrade's story, but nevertheless, it was to be the start of the end for this Hunter Force commander.

As she started to chat, she started to relax and, in doing so, she believed that she had a trusted friend in Shoshanna.

Why would she think otherwise? They were both soldiers. They both killed for a living and both knew the horrors that could follow them around in their roles. It was a moment when Helene thought she could say absolutely anything to Shoshanna without repercussion.

At that time, she could have. But now, as Shoshanna's heart had darkened and pumped the black blood of revenge around her body, the actions she had been told of were not acceptable, not those of a soldier, and no longer honourable.

Helene Marte would not know this then, but she was killing herself slowly with every word of the story she told.

"The operation had gone south; we had lost three men and I was pissed off," she started.

"It was a set up and our Intel had been compromised." Marte was clearly emotional, and benefiting from the chance to open up and get it off her chest. She continued without interruption from Shoshanna.

"When we went in after blowing the wall, the dog was ripped to shreds with machine gun fire. Its body was cut in half; it didn't have time to cry in pain, poor fuck. We got animal guts all over us. It was its job to go in first and it got ripped apart. I have never seen anything like that. They were waiting for us. Waiting, in the fucking empty house we were to use as our staging point."

"Sigmondsen and Harrick were next, caught half way between safety outside and the ambush inside, and, as I saw Sig's head explode and Harry fall, I knew we were fucked."

Shoshanna placed a hand on her fellow soldier's shoulder and encouraged her to keep going, to keep releasing, in the hope she would, perhaps, then move on.

"How the hell any of us got out of that kill zone, I still don't know, but the three of us ran the streets for a while. We hid in and out of the doorways, and shadows. We knew they had watchers, and as you know, Sho, capturing an SF operator alive is a massive prize and kudos for those fuckers. I, for one, didn't want to have my head cut off on prime-time TV. I wasn't ready to die, in that way, that night."

"We got back to a safe house that, this time – I checked first – was safe. We went dark and just waited. No comms and no evac plan, so we just stayed low and waited it out." Marte paused and took another drink of her whisky.

Shoshanna sat close to her. She knew what she had gone through. Many times she herself had escaped death by inches or moments and the fear of imminent death always remains inside the special forces operator. It is just that they are more accustomed to accepting and managing it.

"It was then that we checked our bodies for injury. Adrenalin gone, you know how it is." She paused, which seemed odd to Shoshanna and then she went on without looking at her friend. Instead, Marte looked upwards to the sky – and to the left.

If she knew then what she knew now, then this whole sad story could have been different.

Marte was about to lie, or so it appeared to Shoshanna, adept at reading, and interpreting both body language and inflection.

"They knew we were coming. Someone told them," she started. "Sig and Harrick didn't stand a chance. Like the fuckin' dog, it was a suicide mission as soon as we rolled out. Weirdly, however, Jergson, who was our point man, had stayed back and Johanson, our demolitions man, seemed to have let the blast come out towards us – he hadn't shaped it away. There was something wrong. I know this now, but at the time, it happened so fast."

Shoshanna's face changed. She didn't understand why her friend, sitting in front of her and opening up, a unit commander, would have allowed this strange order to have been carried out. Marte seemed to have no acceptance of blame in her voice.

"We sat and checked our bodies. Armour off, and it was then that we saw both Jerg and Johns were bleeding. Bleeding badly. They reached for their medi-packs and the morphine jab. After that, it was time to dress the wounds and stop the bleeding. I took the lead. When I stitched Johns up and dressed the wound, he fell back and seemed to go into shock. He mumbled out loud, 'Me, I did it, me, I shouldn't have allowed them to go first'."

"This bothered me, but I had Jerg to see to. Then, I seemed to phase out. Have you ever done that, Sho, after a mission come-down?"

Shoshanna said nothing. Instead, she simply kept her stare straight at her commander friend.

"I lost it, Sho. I thought they were going to kill me. I know it makes no sense but it was just a momentary lapse and I now have to live with it."

"Live with what, Helene?"

"I did it. I know the hearing cleared me; but I did it. I shot them both. Single shot through the head to make it look like it was those fuckers we were after and they'd both been executed. I thought someone in my team had betrayed us." Marte paused again and shifted uncomfortably on her seat.

"I thought I had to, in a moment of madness, I had to do it, Sho."

Shoshanna looked away. At that time, many years earlier, she didn't see the whole picture. She didn't see then what she knew for certain now. Helene Marte was the one. She was the one that sent her unit in to die, and when two survived, she did away with them and made up her escape story.

Helene Marte was a traitor and she was still leading men into battle. She was still a risk and now, today, sitting as she was, waiting for her chance to get on board *Dragon*, Shoshanna knew that Marte had to be taken out.

Standing up, Shoshanna went to the small shower room. Now slightly less angry, she stepped in and washed her body clean of all her evil acts, making way for a sinister deed later that night on a Royal Navy vessel called HMS *Dragon*. She would often 'cleanse' her soul of the badness she committed in the name of others, but this night, she also felt anger. She was angry because the shower was not serving its purpose. The water dripping off her body was not washing the evil away, running it down the plug hole. Instead, her skin seemed to be hard and rough, and everything was sticking to her. She would have to start the next attack dirty and angry – something that bothered her greatly as she left the building.

The moon illuminated the Thames River snaking along past the vessel, as it had done so for hundreds of years, for kings and queens, and even before men and women walked the land. Now, the moon lit up the water and the bank, where partygoers and walkers jostled for position on the pathway.

For a fleeting moment, Shoshanna held her position in the water. The currents were strong but she was stronger. She watched the people on the walkways, chatting about their day and their hopes for the night to come. Conversations and laughter carried towards her on the breeze. Turning towards her quest, she allowed the current to carry her down river and towards the sleeping *Dragon*, moored in view of all who came to Greenwich to find solace at the home of time.

She knew she would only have one attempt to grab the mooring, but she would only need one. Her bag, attached to her arm, followed along, floating above the waterline. The balloon was working. It needed to stay dry.

Like all naval vessels in dock, the world over, the moorings are a weak point – they were always guarded. She knew this and was prepared.

As she climbed the thick rope, upwards towards the deck, her hands burned, but she didn't let herself feel it. That was for later. Now, she readied herself.

She was only a few feet from the deck when she pulled the dangling bag up and opened it. Steadying herself on the rope with her legs, she put her hand inside and grabbed the bird. She had secured a pigeon earlier that day, and now, wings clipped and its beak glued together to stop it giving her position away, this simple creature was about to get her on board the most fearsome of vessels, undetected.

She held its wings close to its body. She could feel its heart pounding in its chest. It was about to die, and perhaps, it sensed this, as it tried in vain to let out noise, releasing the pain from its chest and lungs.

Then, without emotion, she threw the bird onto the deck by the mooring and it performed its role admirably.

Stumbling and falling while trying to fly, the pigeon tottered in pain around the deck. Startled, the armed guard stepped back a little and readied his weapon.

"What the fuck," she heard, as she eased her way on board and immediately out of sight below deck. The doomed bird had been a sufficient distraction. The whole action had taken less than thirty seconds and she was now live and making her way to Helene Marte's quarters. Having studied detailed plans of the layout of the vessel, it would be easy for her to quickly get to her target's location.

Meanwhile, the guard had captured the distressed pigeon and, a little bemused, had thrown it back over board to its certain death. It would float downstream along with Shoshanna's plastic covering, now discarded, as it had also served its purpose. She could now walk the tight corridors dry and in uniform, mingling with the on-board crew, who were oblivious to the murder that was minutes away.

She walked past sailor after sailor. All were polite and most let her pass under the tight fire doors first. Some even saluted as they did so. She knew how to manage junior soldiers from her days in active service and would nod firmly but hospitably as she passed by. They would need to believe she was an on-board crew member and a senior one at that.

Along and down she walked until she came to where she needed to be.

Deck sub-three, the drunken sailors from before had said their special guests occupied the starboard side of this level. Marte was in the first cabin. So it was to be – deck three and attack the first cabin, door 2.1.

The energy-saving lights were on. They had picked up her movement along the corridor. She waited and stood still right outside cabin 2.1.

She listened for noise inside and waited for the timer to release the darkness back into the corridor.

It went dark: now motionless, the light sensors believed her gone.

She drew her knife, but this was no ordinary weapon. The blade started with a sharp point but became a thicker serrated lump of steel two centimetres down the shaft. Once the point was in the wound, it allowed the thicker element to slide in easily, yet causing maximum damage.

Shoshanna reached into her chest pocket and pulled out a tiny tube of clear liquid. Botulinum toxin could be lethal if inhaled or it came into contact with human skin. She covered her nose and mouth with a moist cloth, then she dripped the liquid onto the blade, being careful not to get any on her clothing. Then, blade readied, she squirted the tiny tube of liquid onto the cabin door handle. When the body of her target was discovered, a second unsuspecting person would be travelling to their God moments later. The toxic poison was such that death would follow before the recipient had even fallen to the floor.

She needed to be sure. Shoshanna needed to know that her target, her former friend, Helene Marte, the best of the best, would not and could not react, and fight back. Strangely, she did not want her to suffer. Death was good enough. Like after the fight with Vitschencko, she would need to leave the area quickly, making haste to get off the vessel. She calculated she would need four minutes before the bodies would likely be discovered. The poison and the second unfortunate victim would likely do their job by distracting anyone who walked past en route to the medical facility, letting her escape unnoticed.

She now had a sense of urgency about her. Someone could come at any moment, finding her standing alone in the corridor, knife in hand.

The movement of her free arm knocking on the door of cabin 2.1 immediately put the motion-lights back on. Momentarily, Shoshanna was visible and vulnerable – knife in hand, murder imminent.

She had taken a second to accustom herself to the unique sounds of the corridor and this part of the vessel. She had done this well. Now she could hear a new noise; the inhabitant of the cabin moving inside. The noise came closer to the door.

Shoshanna's knife glistened in the down-lighter, with the moist, lethal liquid waiting on its blade. She raised her knife-hand to face-height, her free shoulder readied to force the door if need be.

As the cabin door opened, the flicker and sounds of a television broke the silence in the corridor. Despite her past and her active role in special forces, Helene Marte would never have suspected she was in mortal danger on a Royal Navy destroyer surrounded by two hundred plus British sailors. She was wrong.

For the second that her eyes and brain still functioned, she saw a tall, uniformed woman standing before her in the corridor. Then, the instant the knife entered her left eye, she saw nothing. Her brain stopped and, before the blood could drip off the serrated blade, Helene Marte's body was falling downward, already dead.

The weight of her dying fall pulled the blade back out of her head as Shoshanna held on to it. Her body fell mostly back into the room. Kicking a limp arm inside the swing of the cabin door and, throwing the knife into the room, Shoshanna closed the door, careful not to touch the handle.

Done.

Fuck, that was strange, she thought quietly to herself.

Walking swiftly back, retracing her steps, she checked her uniform for blood splatters.

Out the corridor and through the first fire door. Safe, no one. Two more to go, then up the ladder to the higher deck level.

Fast but not urgent or desperate, she reminded herself.

Her first contact came at the last fire door before the ladder to the floor above.

"Evening, ma'am," said one rating, while the other moved aside to let this female officer upward.

Shoshanna acknowledged them and ascended the ladder, continuing onwards while wondering if one of those junior non-commissioned sailors were to have the fatal pleasure of discovering Marte's body.

Two more fire doors and one more set of stairs until she would see the night sky and breathe fresh air, rather than the recirculated and slightly warm stuff the crew down below endured.

Stars.

"Christ, at last," she said out loud, surprising herself with her lack of caution.

She walked to the shore side of the top deck and stopped. Sensing she was seen, she stretched and pretended to light up a cigarette.

Calm, Sho, they know nothing. Just be cool, girl, she thought to herself, this time silently, as she faced towards the illuminated sails of the *Cutty Sark*. The last tea clipper and once fastest vessel on the oceans, its name came from a short garment worn by a witch from Scottish poetry. Now, as she stood and kept an eye on those who were close, Shoshanna felt like the witch from the poem. She had killed a former friend and stood, in the moonlight, waiting for her opportunity to jump overboard into the cold, fast-flowing currents of the Thames. Overboard, yes, but to safety, away from a body that could be discovered at any moment and the alarm signalled.

The reflection from the moon rippled on the river below her. She had to wait for her moment to jump and it had to be just right. If she failed to balance the movement of the boat against its moorings, while waiting for those on guard to stop noticing her, then she could easily be jumping to her death, crushed by the side of the vessel.

Shoshanna stood and waited. She was getting more and more agitated. The body of her former friend, together with the owner of the first hand to touch the cabin door, could set the strategic operation she was following into a panicked rush at any moment. She waited and occasionally looked over at the two points where she was visible to the ship's guards.

Then as luck had it, she spotted a police patrol vessel close by, slowing. The moored destroyer was clearly a target to anyone who would have a large or sophisticated enough weapon and as a result, the river police patrolled regularly.

This irony – of law enforcement providing her with the chance to escape from the *Dragon* and home to plan her next move – was not lost on her.

As the patrol approached slowly, signalling towards the upper deck, both her potential spotters moved away, and towards their police colleagues bobbing up and down on the currents near the bigger vessel. The hum of their engines would help disguise the noise of her leap into the river.

Focus, Sho, she thought to herself as she dropped the cigarette over the side and placed both hands on the barrier. Then, with one last glance over her shoulder, she flexed both arms and legs, and propelled herself out and down towards the cold water.

She hit the water and went under. Disorientated and unable to see anything through the murky waters, she knew she had to move away from the boat, but she did not yet know which way to go.

Slowly, she regained control, and the air in her lungs started to move her upwards and back to the surface.

As her face broke through to the night air, she inhaled loudly. Suddenly, she saw the massive side of the vessel coming towards her, being moved by the currents. Too late to move away, she braced herself for the impact.

When it struck her on the shoulder and back, she knew instantly that she had been injured and could not survive a second impact.

The massive metal wall that had hit her once and moved her a few feet through the water towards the beach, then turned on the current and moved slowly away from her. It would be back. She had to act now.

Gathering all her reserves of energy, Shoshanna started to swim to the lights of the shore. Relative safety may only have been thirty metres away but the impact had taken its toll on her and the water was cold, very cold. She struggled to use both arms to swim.

It took her a few minutes to reach a point on the shore where she could defeat the currents trying to drag her back in. Then she stood as best as her tired body allowed her to and walked to the shore, onto the wet sand of the river's edge.

"I really don't want to do that again," she whispered out loud, as if expecting an audience to hear her. There was no one nearby, thankfully, just a lone seagull that had made temporary home on the sand and decided it was best to move away.

Shoshanna lay on the wet sand for a few more minutes watching the occasional cyclist and dog walker on the path above her.

Time to go home, she thought as she lifted herself up to her feet and over to the base of the wall with the footpath above her.

She cleared away the wooden debris that she had used to hide a rucksack earlier, and within fifteen minutes, drier and now in warmer civilian clothing, she sneaked back onto the public walkway and towards a taxi rank. She was too tired to walk home that night.

By the time the body of Sub Lieutenant Phillips was pronounced dead in the ship's medical room and the second body of a visiting special forces soldier had set off a ship-wide emergency, Shoshanna was too far away, in the warmth of a London taxi, to hear or see the commotion on board.

This had, indeed, been the hardest target yet and she needed time to recover from her injuries. She was not able to visit a hospital, nor was she able to tell anyone that a Royal Navy destroyer had struck her in the water, causing massive bruising and a dislocation that she would have to force back into place herself when she got home. For now, she simply put up with her pain and chose not to speak to her driver but instead pretended to sleep.

It would be three days later that the local press would eventually get access to report on the incident.

Three days later that her only friend in the world, Lisa, would read that the authorities were looking for a tall, athletic woman who posed as an officer on board a British destroyer docked in Greenwich. A woman reported to have an Israeli or Middle Eastern accent.

Three days later that this same friend would battle her suspicions and come to the conclusion that she did not, in fact, know who this could be. Instead, she would wait for the next time her friend, Shoshanna, would come to town and visit, and tell her of the wonders and excitement of her travels around the planet. Unbeknown to her, this would never happen, but she would wait irrespective.

Three days later, Connor Law would read yet another article whose subject matter was the killing of a special forces soldier. This in itself was not news or uncommon, but for Law, the pattern was suspicious. None had been on active duty; most were, in fact, retired. He could not yet figure out what was linking the deaths, if a link was even truly present. But although he didn't realise it yet, he did indeed know the connection and it would return to his conscious in due course. Shoshanna Agnon and Connor Law had history, and this past would soon enough return to the present.

Chapter 9
Return

Her last target had sent ripples around the special forces fraternity.

Not only was the killing carried out on a military vessel, which should have been secure and safe, but also a pattern seemed to be developing.

News reporters started putting the pieces together, and the conspiracy theorists were dining out on stories and make-believe.

Those inside the secretive world of covert ops took this spate of murders very seriously and began to shut up shop. Someone was after them, and whoever it was, didn't seem to care what nation and which brand of special forces they represented. Worse still, they knew that it was someone capable of getting in and out undetected, the very skill set they held dear and sacred.

Shoshanna monitored the stories and speculation, and took pleasure in the sense of disbelief and confusion.

Perhaps, Marte won't turn out to have been the hardest, she thought to herself as she scanned the latest report on her phone. *Perhaps, they will be more aware now, and getting to him and the others might be harder as they become suspicious of everyone around them?*

"Whatever," she said out loud as her thoughts became words, surprising the pilot of the small fishing boat she was on, now approaching shore.

She had paid the crew to drop her off quietly on the shore of a small fishing village, Bat Yam, just south of Tel Aviv and from there, she would merge into the local population unnoticed, making her way to Jerusalem and her home suburb.

She was around ten minutes from shore when she gathered the three-man crew together and, gun in hand, asked for their mobile phones. None refused.

Phones now sinking down to the seabed, she paid the captain her agreed fee, plus additional Israeli Shekel, so they could go and buy three new phones. She then put a hand on each man's shoulder and thanked them. They stood bewildered. As the harbour came into view, she followed the captain to the controls and, monitoring his radio contact with the harbour masters, allowed him to go about his usual docking procedure. When complete, she cut the power lead to the generator with her knife. An easy repair but an immediate effect.

Shoshanna was back in Israel, and a part of her heavy and dark heart lifted.

She chose to stay the night in Tel Aviv and found cheap accommodation. Dumping her few possessions, she went out into the buzzing night to eat. It would be uneventful, just as she wanted.

Her spirits were lifted still further once her stomach was full, and the noise and smells of her homeland filled her head and her heart.

Her shoulder injury from London had healed well, but there would be forever a small scar from the impact to match the other recent one where the barbed wire from the cage ripped her flesh on the mission before that.

Shoshanna had multiple scars from operational injuries, and each time she saw a new addition, she would smile to herself and think that, one day, she really should count them all.

For now, she put her head down for the night. Tomorrow, she would make her way to Jerusalem and her suburb, where some may still recognise her, but she might not recognise the place that she once called home.

She would wake and start her day long before the sun did. This was normal routine for Shoshanna. Rising before the first rays of sunlight hit the land was what had kept her alive many times in her former career. This was the norm for any special operator who lived for the night and would become wary of the day, when their advantage was taken away from them.

This day, in this land, however, she rose early out of instinct, not fear or necessity. She was as safe as she could be in her homeland, starting the journey to her hometown.

The bus to Jerusalem would be a dull and uneventful trip, but she did not mind this.

The dusty roads and the featureless surroundings would not help. The numerous road blocks and regular passenger checks by armed conscription soldiers would also be a pain, but travelling in her homeland, using her mother tongue and real passport, she would merge in with the other passengers and had nothing to worry about. This would simply be a dull and long journey. A journey during which she hoped she would find out why she felt compelled to take it.

A few hours passed uneventfully. She knew this would be so and had allowed herself to relax into a much needed sleep. When the bus did finally stop, she sprung up in her seat. She had fallen asleep deeper than she expected. Her body and mind clearly needed it. So the sudden stop and the hiss of releasing brake pressure awoke her in a readied-and-fighting state of alert.

As soon as she sprang into action, she realised she had over reacted. Her fellow passengers, now looking directly at her, seemed surprised and bemused.

"Final stop, final stop, Zalman Shazar Central Station. Bags at the front," came across the bus tannoy.

"Christ, I need to stretch," was her response to the bus driver, quietly but out loud to herself.

Shoshanna collected her two shoulder bags from above her seat and made her way out of the bus, into the dust, heat and hustle of busy downtown Jerusalem.

"Food, I need to eat," she said to herself. She had spent so much time on her own that she was using the sound of her voice to keep herself company.

This was yet another thing she learned during survival training in Shayetet 13. If it is safe to do so, tell yourself out loud what you must do. This would keep the brain positive and the heart believing that it was not alone. For now, she spoke out loud, for she was lonely but didn't fully know it.

Her stomach full of fried artichokes and herring bread, she paid the waiter, and set off towards her parents' home and a meeting with her memories. She did not yet know why she was compelled to go there, but compelled she was.

Her parents' former home was close – her former home – and while it was a place of safety and security as she was growing up, it also had a dark and cold side that made Shoshanna hesitant about going closer.

The memories came flooding back when she sat on the wall and stared at the 'for sale' sign at the end of the short driveway. She had heard from a former army colleague that her father had died soon after her mother and that she was now alone in the world. Strangely, she was always alone in this life and while the news saddened her, she had been expecting it.

Despite her determination not to cry, she found her eyes filling with tears. "Stop crying, you fool, it's only a house." Shoshanna wiped the falling tears from her cheek and moved off the wall towards the building.

With a bag across both shoulders to help hide her face from one-time neighbours, she walked up through the lawn, remembering the last time she was there.

She remembered her father's celebration of her joining Shayetet 13 and how she had to sneak into the kitchen to speak with her mother. A mother she had not seen in weeks but had to steal away to embrace, so as not to embarrass her father in front of his friends.

She wondered to herself, as she walked, if she was hiding her face to conceal her identity from her former neighbours, avoiding any awkward contact, or so they would not see her cry.

As she approached the side of the house, she stopped and looked over into the nearby field. The horse was still alive and still grazing but a little slower than she remembered. She remembered hearing the sound of the helicopter landing, scaring the horse and forcing it to scamper to a faraway corner. In her mind's eye, she saw the dust blow up and her mother, hand over her face, peer through her fingers, watching and sadly waiting for this mechanical flying machine to take her precious daughter away. She remembered leaving the family home for the very last time on a helicopter, with her parents walking away into the house and not looking back as it ascended. Perhaps, they knew it was the end and the final time they would be together. Perhaps, they were just battle-hardened and used to it. Her father surely was, but Shoshanna wondered about her mother's thoughts that day.

Her mother had suspected then, but could never have known for sure, that this helicopter ride would take her daughter away for the last time, never to be seen again. She did not, however, anticipate that she would die first, never to see her daughter or husband again. She had always envisaged her military daughter dying before her, the agony of every mother and that knock on the door of the family home by a man in uniform.

Shoshanna stood a few yards away from the only home she ever knew. She had as many bad memories of living there as good ones, but it was her only family home. Now, as she stood facing the front door, she let the bags drop to the wooden decking.

She closed her eyes, and let herself listen to the noises and felt the breeze on her face. Everything seemed to return to her soul quickly.

At first, she could hear the birds and vehicles moving around her. Then came the engine noise of a plane overhead and in the distance a car horn sounded. But soon, she heard a child's giggles and a mother's laughter. She could hear the voice of a man and the chink of glass on glass. She could smell her mother's cooking over the breeze and finally, she could hear her heart thumping inside her chest. For a moment, Shoshanna was back home. For a few minutes more, she was a young girl playing in her parents' garden and, for still a moment longer, she was happy. Perhaps, the happiest she had been in years. She didn't want the feeling to end but knew that it must. She knew she had to return to the world she lived in now. Reluctantly opening her eyes, the young child she once knew and the happy memories disappeared in a whisper. She was back. She was back in her world of grey and dark, and death.

She walked up to the window near the front door and tried to look in. It was partly boarded up, but she could see the stairs and the corridor that led to the kitchen. Looking back at her bags and believing them to be safe where they fell, she walked around the corner and onto the side decking. It creaked as she stepped on it.

As she walked towards the back door, which looked like it had been secured shut, she heard a footstep close by.

"It's empty," said a voice. There was a pause as Shoshanna flinched and half-cocked her head, rapidly assessing her options. "There's nothing of value in there for you to waste your time with," came next.

As Shoshanna turned towards the voice, she realised that her guard had dropped. Someone had got up close to her and she hadn't seen them first. She had relaxed too much and for her, that was just too dangerous.

"Oh, hello, I'm not looking to steal anything," she said first as she tried to push her memories aside to focus on the old man standing in front of her.

"You see, I am just looking to move into the area and was told this was for sale," she continued, trying to divert any possible recognition.

"Right, of course, you are. In these parts, empty sale houses tend to be shown by the agent. He not available for you today?" the old man retorted, moving even closer to Shoshanna and looking her directly in the eye.

It's Benjamin, Benjamin Abiydan, she thought. *Father's friend from years back. Christ, he might give me away.*

Shoshanna was moments away from being recognised and her disappearance from the military without permission would be blown wide open. She could have the whole country searching for her. She had some sort of anonymity, spread from the word of mouth that she had been captured and tortured, and was likely buried in a shallow grave somewhere in Syria. The next few seconds would be crucial. She had to think quickly.

"So, sir, could you show me around this house? Would that be possible today?" she asked, hoping to defuse his suspicions and remove the incriminating stare from her.

"If I were to see inside and then, perhaps, chat to you about the area, that would be a great help," she continued, turning away from his gaze and looking back towards the house as she slowly walked further round the decking.

"This be the Agnon's old place. It's been run down and empty for a while now. Don't seem the right place for a young single woman like you," he said as he started to walk behind her.

"Not suitable, that is unless you knew them folks. Did you – did you know the Agnons?"

Was this a genuine question or a challenge because he recognised her? Her pulse grew quicker as she pondered.

Shoshanna's brain was working in overdrive. Sure, she could eliminate the old man, her former family friend and hide the body sufficiently for her to leave the area, undiscovered, but this wasn't really a good option.

What to do? she wondered to herself.

"The Agnons were mighty fine, they were. Well, senior and that young girl Shoshanna were, at least," he said and not waiting for her to acknowledge or respond, he carried on.

The next words he spoke told her that he knew her. Told her that she had been recognised and told her that she could no longer talk her way out of it.

"That wife of them lovely Jewish family, that Syrian woman, she brought death to the door of this home. Course, you didn't know them, did you?" But before he could place a hand on her shoulder and directly challenge her, she responded.

With a kick of her boot back behind her into the protruding shin of her former neighbour, she heard a snap of bone and then a massive exhalation of air from his lungs.

Now he was bent double and could not see her face. This was best, for her eyes had returned to their usual blood-red anger. The kick was followed with a full-hand slap to the right side of his head. Slamming into his ear, he was immediately disorientated. He fell to the ground unconscious. When he woke, he would do so in extreme pain, not likely to ever walk properly again.

As Shoshanna walked away from the property at speed, both bags once again over her shoulders partly concealing her face, she knew two things for certain:

She was most likely going to be a local news item and her future movements might be traced; and secondly, she had to get back to London and into the British Foreign Office, quickly, before she was exposed and her trail followed.

She had her next target. She'd had lots of time to determine her list of potentials on the train back from Kazakhstan and now a British former colleague would face her wrath.

She would have less time to plan now that she would probably be on the radar of every law enforcement agency in the world. Soon enough, they would piece the jigsaw of deaths together and come to the conclusion that the numerous special forces deaths were, in fact, carried out by one of their own.

Right here and right now, she had a couple of hours to get out of Israel before things would start to get tough.

"Back to London then, but no friend and no fun this time," she said out loud as she walked the tree-lined street towards the train station and the airport. "This time, it's serious."

Chapter 10
Office

It was another uneventful plane journey back to London, under the guise of different passports. The plane was full of tourists, with the inevitable babble of small children ever present. When it landed, after circling for a while in the London air-traffic stack, Shoshanna retrieved another passport to hand as she stood in line waiting at border control.

She was adept at not standing out from a crowd. She had been taught by the best all her military career. She could hide in plain sight and, yet, she knew that no plan survived the first bullet, so she was ready for action at all times. Her skill set remained true to her today in the long queue of returning tourists, tanned and tired, and already feeling like they needed another holiday.

"Where have you travelled from?" asked the border official as he reviewed Shoshanna's passport.

"Frankfurt," she replied, deliberately smiling at the young child pulling faces at the official in the next booth. She knew it would make her appear more usual and conformist. She had no time for disobedient children but this one served a purpose.

"And the purpose of your visit there was, exactly?" the official continued, his gaze returning from her to his screen.

"I was visiting friends," she replied, turning her own view from the child to the official, as well as downward to his screen as best as she was able.

"Enjoy London," the guard quipped as he handed her back her third fake passport of the journey, which had turned the scanner green, signalling no danger. Because she knew she would get into the country easily, her pulse hadn't quickened, so she simply picked up her rucksack and took the passport.

Again it was raining. *This place! It's always bloody raining,* she thought to herself as she felt the drizzling patter on her upturned face.

Within the hour, she had checked into her bed and breakfast, and was locked away in her room. Another dull and non-descript space in another less than desirable part of London. Opening the small solitary window to determine her position and check for any vulnerabilities, she inhaled the smells and sounds of the city. The black cabs jostled with each other in the streets, seemingly competing with the red buses, and helmeted cyclists risking life and limb trying to beat both vehicle types to their destinations.

Shoshanna lay down on the single bed. She had positioned a chair under the door handle to stop any forced entry, so she felt safe enough for now. Closing her eyes, she allowed herself to sink into a semi-conscious state. London always brought back thoughts of her one true friend, Lisa, but this time, she would not see her. She tried in vain to remember Lisa's mobile phone number, which she had so quickly deleted several days earlier.

She slept. She had not properly slept in a while, but this afternoon, in this rundown, and cheap bed and breakfast, Shoshanna slept. Her mind and body needed this chance to recuperate, and she chose to let it happen.

When she eventually woke, it was because of the noise of a police car wailing past the building at speed, sirens briefly lighting up the Artex ceiling. She had slept through the planes overhead, and the revving cars and buses just below her first-floor window, but instinctively, she woke with the sound of law enforcement.

Christ, it's late, she thought to herself. Her watch said 8.42 am, but this was late for an early riser like Shoshanna. She would often rise and start her day as partygoers were finishing theirs. This morning, however, she woke later than she would wish to but, at least, refreshed.

As she prepared to leave her room and set off in search of something to eat, she crunched up a tiny piece of paper and then carefully positioned it inside the room behind the door. Once she had closed the door behind her, she took out her knife and nudged the paper wad closer to the inside of the door. She had nothing to steal and nothing to give her away. There was no maid service, so if the innocuous looking ball of paper was not in exactly the same place on her return, she would know someone had entered the room and shown an interest in her.

Turning her attention to the lift, she sent it up a couple of floors from her position and then walked down the emergency exit stairs and out quickly, into the hustle of the London streets. The process would be reversed on her return. She would normally have left the television on low in the room – so, from the corridor, it would appear someone was inside – but her current lodgings were too cheap to have such a luxury. Her instinctive routine had kept her safe all over the world and it would do so again in London.

After grabbing a quick bite from a nearby bakery, she took a short bus ride and was soon walking down Petty France Street, which ran parallel to Wellington Barracks, where it seemed to her, a lifetime ago, she and her troop were once made welcome. Not anymore. She was now the enemy.

Crossing over and into St James's park, her day commenced for real. She had started to recce her route into and perhaps, even out of, her target building. It would, however, be a couple of days of planning and watching until she went it. The surveillance was crucial, if often dull, but it was a necessary step in preparing for a kill. She would spend most of the day sitting, and watching the comings and goings, in and out of the Foreign Office, a little way from the park adjoining that seat of British power, the home of the prime minister.

Can't get any closer to the top brass than this, she thought as she opened her water, and sat watching the tourists and civil servants going about their business. Today, it was not raining in London. A fact not missed by Shoshanna as she sat and drank, blending seamlessly into the crowds of visiting tourists. Cameras would click and video would be taken all around her as the mass of London's tourists went about their way, often aimlessly but usually innocently.

The Foreign Office was a very grand and beautiful-looking building, and had been the true seat of British influence around the world centuries back. Today, it struggled with what is asked of it. The rooms were no longer fit for purpose, with today's demands and the numbers of bodies that needed them. The corridors went for miles and the room-numbering system was so illogical, it was as if they knew she was coming and were trying to confuse her. Beautiful and grand it may be, but for the mix of private contractors, civil servants and career politicians who had to work there, it was a place that struggled to serve purpose.

Indeed, for Kyle Scott, it was much better to conduct his business in the privately kept upstairs room above The Clarence public house. The staff knew the Foreign Office regulars and opened the upstairs only for them. Classified conversations would abound in this room, but the universal need for security somehow negated the need for those who met there to keep their conversation quiet.

This was a typical quirk of British politics. A long time ago, the Foreign Office had muscled out its sister, the Ministry of Defence, from The Clarence pub and forced them to have their own private 'chat room' in the Red Dragon public house, weirdly right across from the Foreign Office.

Kyle Scott would conduct his required internal meetings, and then exit the grand old building to further his purpose and position, in The Clarence of Whitehall. Most private contractors preferred meeting in similar public buildings, saying pleasantries to the near-retirement-age guards on the security gate as they left.

It had been four hours since she first sat and watched, and now, having occasionally moved around the park, with the Foreign Office always in sight, she walked past the staff entrances a few times. She had done enough for the first day, she thought, as she peered inside as inconspicuously as she could to gauge security. Guards were everywhere and she could not risk being seen in the area too often. She was a master at moving undetected and between the timing blind-spots of circulating cameras, but even she was getting tired and was aware that she could slip up. For now, she decided to head back to her accommodation.

In happier times, it would be right about now that she would have called her friend for company, but, by her own design, she was unable to enjoy this comfort. Shoshanna decided instead to walk the short distance to where she would sleep, once again, that night.

Tomorrow would be much the same as today. Much the same boredom. Soon enough, it would be tougher than just sitting in the sun, and watching people come and go. Soon, Shoshanna would do the watching and planning from the inside of the secure building.

Shoshanna rose the next day before the sun. She was back to her usual routine. No long sleep for her, but she had her game face on and her mind-set fixed.

"The ship was tough, Sho, but now you need to go further, girl, and infiltrate the heart of British Government," she said out loud as she exited her cheap B&B, small crushed-up piece of paper again positioned directly behind her room door.

As she walked across the street slowly filling up with vehicles and pedestrians, she looked skyward. *Three days on the trot, sun and no rain, thank God*, she thought to herself with habitual, focused determination. She laughed briefly as she thought of the incongruity of thanking any God for her life, as it had been, thus far, full of violence and slaughter. Today, Shoshanna wore a tailored, short summer dress and looked like a woman with a purpose. Not the mercenary more accustomed to carrying weapons than jewellery. Today, she was a lady on a mission, designed to fit in with the business types entering and exiting the Foreign Office, a distance along Whitehall and the neighbour of Number 10 Downing Street.

She would need help getting in, but it didn't take too long before she identified the group that would unknowingly facilitate her entry. Closely following two women and one older, taller man past the initial bag search, the guard clearly assumed they were together as he directed them inside the first gate and towards the second via the visitor reception.

"Seems we have nothing to hide," said Shoshanna, smiling jovially at the group she now walked with. She needed to befriend the threesome if at all possible. The bag search was the easy part. As luck would have it and luck would often be the ally of a special forces warrior, her friendly positioning elicited the response she needed.

"Yes, my dear," said the tall man. "If only they knew, they wouldn't let us lot in!" The other ladies in the party acknowledged his joke with a conspiratorial laugh.

She wanted to be seen talking to them as she entered the reception.

"We all have secrets, don't we?" Shoshanna's retorted. "I wonder what secrets this lovely place has?" she chanced next, as she entered the reception area, conveniently behind the tall man. She touched his arm and smiled at him as he approached the reception desk, hoping that it was seen by the staff behind it. She need not worry.

With one ear on the tall man, Shoshanna took a step away and towards a second receptionist who was waiting to check the meeting list, and print a visitor pass.

"Sir, who are you here to see?" she heard as she stalled, pretending to be retrieving something crucial from her handbag.

She listened intently while smiling at the lady behind the desk.

"Morning, we are here to meet with Robert Colley in CT Middle East section," he said, loud enough to be heard by the receptionist who was still waiting for Shoshanna to state her intentions. *This is too easy*, thought Shoshanna, trying not to look too pleased with herself and her ease of entry.

"Hello, how are you this morning… this *sunny* morning?" Shoshanna said to her receptionist.

"Fine, madam, thank you and are you with this party?" came next as Shoshanna looked over to the tall man, who was now turning away to allow one of the other ladies to provide their name to the reception desk.

"Yes, Rob Colley in CT, my name's Dana Kelso," she replied. Then, before the receptionist could question her as to why there was no visitor named Kelso on the list, she continued. Slightly turning away from the other two ladies, to avoid them hearing, she said, "I trust my office put me on your list, last minute? I didn't think I was going to make this meeting with my colleagues, but here I am." A prolonged smile and a direct stare later, the printer sprang into life.

The receptionist had clearly believed her story. Shoshanna took the pass gratefully and turned towards the entrance she had, moments earlier, walked in through. Then, stepping towards the tall man, she made one last convincing gesture. Again, she put a gentle hand on his arm and spoke, "Yup, nothing to hide." Then, in a quiet voice, she said, "thank you," in response to his smile. "Have a great meeting," she beamed, disengaging herself from the group of three. They had now served their purpose and were needed no more.

Walking towards the second guard, behind the larger and more intimidating gate, she smiled and produced the pass she had just received, before placing it upon the bar-code reader. The turnstile gate made a noise and the red light turned green. In she went.

There was one final task to be completed before Shoshanna was free to seek out her target.

"No breakfast… Is the coffee shop this way?" she said to the guard, who she saw had been captivated by her big and provocative smile. She knew that her visitor pass meant she had to be escorted around the building by a sponsor, but she had no time for it. Instead, Shoshanna moved into the guard's personal space, allowing him to feel her breathing and, she hoped, be distracted.

"Yes, madam," he stammered, as he turned his head towards one corner of the rectangle building. His face was a little red from the encounter.

Walking off, her smile disappeared. *That was easier than I expected*, she thought to herself.

She headed for the staff canteen in the south wing, where just one hundred years earlier, the affairs of the Commonwealth were controlled and imposed. She had done her research. She knew this was not where her target was, but this wing allowed access to the roof and, ultimately, the rest of the building. More specifically, the part of the building that remained anonymous to the public and, to a great extent, most of the civil servants working legitimately inside. It was where he worked, so Shoshanna needed to find it.

The south wing didn't have an elevator. It was the only corner not to have one. It meant that she could not access a floor map of the departments. She needed a plan and she needed a green-coloured pass so she would not be challenged as she walked around unescorted.

Receiving her coffee, she sat down at a table in the staff canteen and watched the other customers, looking for a chance to further exploit her good fortune.

As visitors and staff came, and left, Shoshanna would move positions to try to get close to a 'look-alike' woman who held a green pass. This was no easy matter, requiring two further refills of coffee. Then, when it happened, it did so very quickly.

A chance handbag left unattended, a simple diversionary move towards the victim's table guest and it was taken. Now she had a green pass in her possession, she needed to act quickly. She knew she had, perhaps, one hour, maximum, before the pass would be made invalid when discovered lost.

She left her coffee on the table and walked quickly up the nearby marble staircase. She was now searching for the 'deniable' section. The place of secret Foreign Office activities – their very existence 'denied'. It was where 'he' worked: the part of the building which never showed up on any Google map searches. Hidden from public view, the deniable section was her target and to reach it, she knew only that she needed to go up. Up as far as she could and, perhaps, to the roof.

The next sixty minutes were going to be challenging; she had no formulated plan, no exact idea where she was going and still no certainty that she would be able to get close to her target. The next hour could be her hardest yet.

Kyle Scott sat and tapped on the keyboard. He sat at the computer for long periods most days, collecting geospatial data on hostile countries and searching endlessly for infill locations for British special forces. A senior analyst, he had the ear of the highest ranking British officers and with this, their trust.

Scott was cleared to the highest security level and had, on many occasions, been privy to live kill-operations and deniable enemy renditions on lands some would be unable to place on a map of the world. He had seen Shoshanna before. He had seen her and her small troop a few times, but hadn't a clue that one of the moving figures, visible through thermal imaging, was a female operative. He could not have known that the soldier he had witnessed on large secure screens deep down under Whitehall, would come back to meet him, with vengeance in her heart.

Shoshanna had a long memory, and his lack of care and attention earlier in her military career was still fresh in her mind. She had barely survived the helicopter crash in which the rest of her team had perished. The landing point had been badly judged and the enemy was waiting to ambush her team. She survived the crash, but it took much more for her to endure the months of torture in captivity. He should have done better; he should have seen the infill point had been compromised. He had sent them in like lambs to the slaughter. Shoshanna had a long memory and as she moved upwards towards the deniable section, Kyle Scott tapped away on his keyboard.

The highest floor in the building was the fourth. Her target would definitely be on the highest floor. This level also had additional security, which she had to bypass. If she was even able to overcome the optical and full-body scanners and pass through CCTV, then she would be closer to her mark, but she'd still have to deal with the digital fingerprint identification. Finally, there would be the others, already sitting at their desks, tapping away on keyboards.

The deniable section rarely had visitors in summer dresses. They were more used to unshaven, swearing soldiers, returning from secret operations, who liked to let every civilian know that they didn't have a paymaster. The soldiers enjoyed levelling expletive filled conversations towards the analysts, who would sit and take the intimidation. What else could they do?

Fourth floor.

She had followed a woman into the corridor and deliberately fumbled in her handbag, searching for a non-existent mobile phone, allowing the other woman to pass the optical scanner first. The door opened and in she went, not holding it for Shoshanna. The door had to open, and close for each and every staff member so the system could maintain an account of people's movements and location.

As it swung towards close, Shoshanna trapped it slightly open with her foot. As quick as she did this, she moved her foot away and allowed it to seal shut.

Too hard, she thought. Fearing her luck would not hold for a further three 'rounds' of security measures, she temporarily retreated and considered her options.

She withdrew further back, into the ladies toilet she had just passed in the corridor and sat in a cubicle to think.

It was, perhaps, several minutes later that good fortune came knocking again.

The Foreign Office is situated only yards from the prime minister's residence and even closer to that of the British chancellor. The chancellor, Philip Tailor, had brought his cat, 'Petra', with him when he moved cabinet roles. Petra was known by all the Foreign Office staff. She would wander across the internal courtyard towards the canteen and wait for her usual morning treat from visitors. They thought it a topic of conversation that a cat could wander freely through the strict security set-up. The same cat was also known to breach the exterior walls and enter the deniable area, much to the amusement of those inside, who had such rigid procedures to adhere to.

So, as Shoshanna contemplated her next move, in the cubicle, on the top floor of a government secure building, Petra came in through a ventilation window and introduced herself. Petra really was indeed an excellent climber.

In that moment, Shoshanna had her plan.

The Foreign Office never closed, but it did empty of most staff in the early evening. Realising her stolen green pass may not be needed any further, she decided to sit it out and wait until most over-paid private contractors got lazy, and joined the lower-paid civil servants calling it a day.

It was another hot afternoon in London, something that would prove to be integral to her plan.

Like many old buildings, designed for a few and now occupied by many, the Foreign Office lacked air-conditioning. The upside of this was that windows would be open. Petra had led the way and who would expect a female assassin, hiding in a toilet in a secure government building, to exploit the same weakness?

She sat a while and listened to staff exchanging pleasantries as they left the building. It was six thirty and very few people remained on the fourth floor. She decided the time was now.

Shoes off, she exited the cubicle in the same manner that the cat had entered, although she did have to unscrew the swing window to make the area large enough for her. Expertly walking the narrow ledge, she quickly bypassed the optical scanners and electromagnetic sensors. There were cameras around the building but she could see that all were pointing downward towards the courtyard. In less than one minute, she was next to an open window, which she determined was big enough for her to enter.

Wait, Sho, must be certain, she thought as she steadied herself, holding her breath and listening acutely. She slowly peered inside at the rows of empty computers. At the very end of the long room were two people, but they seemed to be chatting socially and not paying any attention to the rest of the room. *It has to be now, now, come on, Shoshanna*, she thought to herself, knowing she had a limited time to make her move.

She carefully placed a hand on the open window and moved her body closer into position. As she did, her feline visitor from earlier suddenly reappeared. This time, both human and cat were surprised, and Petra reacted aggressively. Instinct took over for both of them.

Petra hissed with anger, while Shoshanna's reaction was to reach out and silence the animal. The hiss would be short lived.

Grabbing the cat face on, her hand engulfing its whole head, Shoshanna squeezed hard. She could feel the vibrations of the squeal, now being muffled in her hand. Pulling the cat closer and re-securing her position on the window ledge, she placed its body tight onto her leg and, with one violent twist, broke Petra's neck. The vibration stopped. In one ruthless moment, she had reverted back to her instincts and her training. *If it poses a danger or can reveal a position, the target must be eliminated.* This maxim was as much true for a friendly cat as it was for a human foe.

The cat tumbled lifelessly down the four floors into the courtyard. She would, no doubt, be found next morning and reported dead, having fallen from a height on one of her many climbing expeditions across the capital's government buildings. Not many people do an autopsy on a cat.

Shoshanna went inside, the two office officials now closer towards the door into the corridor beyond and, hopefully, soon, on their way out of the building.

Scott, bloody Scott. Where the fuck are you? Shoshanna's mind raced as she scanned the row of name plates from desk to desk.

The two workers were still socialising, but Shoshanna was now much closer to them.

There!

'Kyle Scott – Senior CT Analyst' it read.

Within seconds, she retrieved the spray taped between her breasts and very carefully opened it. Placing one hand over her nose and mouth, she gently squirted its contents all over the keyboard.

As quickly as she had arrived, she left, retracing her route back along the rows of workstations, through the window, dead cat many metres below her and back along the ledge into the familiar toilet cubicle.

With the window back in place and shoes on, Shoshanna needed to exit fast.

As she stood in front of the mirror and straightened her hair, she noticed a reddening mark beginning to appear between her breasts where she had ripped the tape off rapidly a few minutes earlier. She then quickly left the bathrooms and retraced her steps back through the building, then down in the lift, and out and down the marble staircase.

The staff canteen was closing up for the night and the economy-saving lighting was now on for the evening. This subdued illumination would facilitate her quick retreat.

It was evening but it was still warm in the London night. Shoshanna did not look out of place with her summer dress and small handbag. She walked back out into the courtyard, where hours earlier she had mingled with those walking and chatting, clutching coffees and papers as they went about their business. Now, she cut a solitary figure, in her little dress, walking towards the exit gate and the security guards.

"Working late, ma'am?" asked one guard as she approached. She could see that they were not the same guards from earlier.

"Yup, North Korea as usual, you know…" she replied, trying hard not to make too much eye contact.

Then, as she went to raise her pass to the security reader, anxious and wondering if it would even work, the second guard spoke.

"Madam, are you ok? I sense you're troubled," he said in a manner that showed no concern at all for her well-being. She realised it was a subtle challenge. In a building where much work is shrouded in secrecy, she realised she had offered too much by way of explanation for her lateness.

Think, think, don't mess up now, you're almost there, Shoshanna thought as she steeled herself for the act.

"Yes, fine," she replied as breezily as possible, fighting the urge to elaborate with some made-up story about her day.

Shoshanna readied herself for a fight and a quick exit if need be. She knew he had picked up on something, but as her anxiety grew, he appeared to back down.

She raised her stolen pass to the reader.

Green light.

She held her breath as the gate made a recognisable unlocking noise. She walked forward, pushing it open.

As she walked through, free to escape, the second guard spoke again.

"Have a safe night, Miss Durnin." And, caught by surprise, Shoshanna stalled for a split second wondering who the hell Durnin might be.

Then she figured it out – her stolen pass.

"Thanks, guys, have a quiet night, see you tomorrow," she replied as casually as possible before walking out towards Whitehall. She would not see them tomorrow. She would, however, see *him*.

As Shoshanna walked out and into the street, she could not stop herself smiling. The purported headquarters of the world's seat of secrecy had just been penetrated by one sole female operator, to devastating consequence for one of its highest serving members of staff. One sole female assassin and a now dead cat.

Chapter 11
Retribution

She lay in wait. Like a cat waiting for the mouse to come back out from its hiding hole and run the gauntlet once again, she waited for him.

Standing under the security cameras and across from the exit of the Foreign Office, Shoshanna waited.

The poison would first make its victim dizzy. A short while later, it would result in stomach cramps and these would get more painful as the toxin took hold of the victim's organs. When it started to close the organs down, these stomach cramps would become increasingly agonising.

Death would come within forty-eight hours after contact with the barely visible liquid Shoshanna had sprayed on the keyboard. The poison was not officially known to Western medicine and, as of yet, had no cure. The same poison proved very useful to special operators when they needed information from the target but not their immediate death. The promise of a cure would encourage even the most hardened subject to reveal their secrets before their inevitable death.

Watching from a location out of sight of the security cameras, Shoshanna waited for Kyle Scott to exit, not long after she had watched him enter and joke with the gate guards.

Sure enough, she had been waiting only forty minutes when Scott wandered out of the building and walked quite slowly towards Westminster Underground Station. Clearly unaware of the extent of his illness, he had simply decided to leave and make his own way home, hopeful he would recover from what must no doubt be a nasty bug. What did he eat yesterday? He ran his mind over the previous day's meals to try to identify a potential culprit.

She followed him a short distance.

111

When he stopped and lunged his left hand towards a wall for support, she knew for sure that the poison was starting to take hold. She may not have as much time as she had previously imagined, so instead of following him home, she decided to confront him there and now.

"Sit down, Kyle Scott," Shoshanna said, as she stood in his way. Scott looked back at the tall figure blocking his sunlight, clearly puzzled.

"Sit down, Scott. We need to chat," she said, indicating to the small wall next to the pavement.

Still puzzled, he sat down on a protruding part of the wall. Shoshanna knelt very close, next to him.

"My name is Agnon. But you won't remember or care about that. What you will care about is that the dizzy spells and the stomach cramps are just the start."

Confounded by the confrontation, Scott tried to speak, but Shoshanna interrupted him.

"La Ciudad Perdida. Columbia. Do you remember?" she said, directly facing Scott. "The helicopter crash. All your fucking fault. Remember?"

Shoshanna made to continue. Scott knew she had more to say and anyway, he was racking his mind trying to recollect the location just divulged, along with her identity.

Exactly as he remembered the mission he led from the operations room, she spoke again. This time more forcefully.

"I survived the crash. I even survived being captured and tortured by those fuckers we went after; you must have known they were all over the place. Now, I am here and you need to know that I will survive longer. Longer than you."

Scott groaned as a wave of pain came across him and seemed to settle in his stomach.

"I survived but the others were not so lucky. You messed up badly that day, Scott."

Scott looked away from her glare. He now remembered. He remembered it all; he didn't even sanction a secondary team to go in and attempt a rescue. He looked back at her with a mix of fear and trepidation. The pain and now this news, were too much for him to comprehend.

"Now, my team missed out on watching their kids grow up, laughing with them, family stuff. So will you, Scott. The pain you are feeling is bitrixomal 377. It's a poison that, as you sit there, is starting to shut your body down."

Shoshanna stood up, no longer threatening; she was enjoying having the upper hand and her little slice of vengeance. Vengeance for herself and her three lost friends.

"You may have thirty-six hours left. There is no cure, but you already know that. If you have kids, Scott, I suggest you skip the hospital and go see them. Say goodbye. Tell them you love them. Tell them all the things that my dead troop were robbed of the opportunity to do. You have a second chance." Shoshanna smiled and lifted his chin with her hand. "Do it, but do it quick."

With that, she turned and walked away. She would end up at her cheap bed and breakfast soon enough, but for now, Shoshanna turned towards Whitehall and walked in the direction of the Clarence public house.

Scott stood, clasping his stomach; he waved away a bystander who saw he was suffering. Instead, he hailed a black London cab. He would enter the cab and instruct the driver to speed towards a certain private primary school, where he would take his young boy out of class and home early.

Chapter 12
Revive

A few days later, Shoshanna passed through security, without a hitch, at London City Airport and waited to board her plane. She bought several broadsheet newspapers in which she was looking for one specific item, in one specific location. Closure required her to read the obituary columns and seek out a specific name – Kyle Scott.

She was changing. She knew she was changing, but she was also afraid to fully acknowledge or accept it. She was tired of her lifestyle, of her existence and of all the killing. She was growing up and growing weary of it.

On occasions, she would float away into her imagination and back to that beach where she had taken him those many years ago. Their private island and their private stretch of sand. The place where two battle-hardened and bloodied warriors could drop the armour and the tough façade, and simply be two lovers together; vulnerable, exposed but happy. Mostly, just happy.

Now, boarding a plane in London, she was going back there. It would be many hours of travel later, but then, she would be back at her special idyll.

She wondered what sort of reception it would give her now and, indeed, what sort of memories would come back to her. She knew she needed to be there. It was all too much – the cage, the fighting and the ship – it was all getting too much for her body and mind, and she needed the recharge.

Shoshanna's destination: a secluded beach community in Tombua, Angola. By nightfall, she would know if she had done the right thing by returning there. For now, she sat at the rear of the plane and sipped her second neat whisky while she searched for the name.

When the food trolley started its slow, methodical journey down the aisle, Shoshanna was first to receive the choice.

"Madam, the chicken or the vegetarian option?"

"Chicken please and can I have two more miniature whiskies?" she replied politely to the crew member.

"Certainly," responded the stewardess as she bent to retrieve the food. As she came back up, tray in hand and prepared to hand it over to Shoshanna, she paused, puzzled. Whereas a second ago she faced a polite and smiling customer, now the casually dressed lady seemed to wear an expression far more sinister. Shoshanna was still smiling but in a whole new manner, which initially startled the crew member.

One newspaper carried the name Kyle Scott in its obituary column. He had died of causes unknown. Thirty-eight thousand feet above the ground, Shoshanna's half-smile, half-sneer made the staff member uncomfortable. For Shoshanna alone knew the cause of death.

The plane landed on time in the capital, Luanda. As Shoshanna inhaled deeply on exiting the aircraft door, she knew she was certainly no longer in London. The heat and humidity struck her face as she descended the few stairs down to the tarmac.

Security showed the same lax standards that she remembered from a while back. The guards were poorly paid and it was custom to 'support' their families by placing the local kwanza currency inside the passport when handing it over.

How much went in and was handed over determined how easy passport control was for the traveller. Shoshanna knew this and so, to expedite her onward journey to her beach of memories, she placed five thousand kwanza into the passport, which now bulged. Using both hands to keep it secure, she handed it over.

Within moments, the passport was handed back to her unchecked. It had taken the border guard several seconds to collect up all the notes. She moved on towards the taxi rank.

Luanda was the most expensive city in Africa, now that the civil war had ended, and divided the city into haves and have nots. Sitting on billions of dollars of oil reserves, the lucky few now navigated their super yachts through the rubbish and litter of the shanty towns. Shoshanna had arranged a meeting but it was not towards the 'haves' that she directed the taxi driver. She wanted him to go into the heart of the shanty town high up on the hill, ironically, with the best views of the rich and sprawling capital city.

"No go there, madam, danger," said the driver in his best English. Shoshanna replied in Portuguese, and for the next minute, the two would argue the price and drop-off location. The deal done, the taxi set off. Twenty minutes later, Shoshanna was duly dropped off. Swinging her rucksack onto her back, she set off deep into the shanty town and to her rendezvous.

All eyes on me, she thought, as she walked the mud and broken tarmac roads past open corrugated iron and wood homes. "Keep aware, Sho," she would say to herself while trying to look as if she knew exactly where she was going. She knew that in this environment, she stood out like a sore thumb and that people would inevitably be watching.

Her contact would make himself known to her once she appeared in the open square in the centre of this most temporary-looking of neighbourhoods. For now and without a weapon, her only defence was her experience and her hand-to-hand combat ability if someone were to try to steal her possessions, or worse, try to kidnap her for sexual favours followed by a bullet to the head.

Her contact had informed her that the square was close to a tall church tower, and that she should be able to catch glimpses of it through and above the homes. As it came in and out of view, Shoshanna became a little less worried that she was being fooled and walking into a trap. After all, a white woman travelling alone would be a valuable target for the gangs that ran the shanty town – doubly so for the package she was after. She also knew that the local police would not bother to risk their own lives to save a foreigner who wanted to purchase a weapon.

When she walked out into the square and towards a small café, however, Shoshanna felt more vulnerable than she had when navigating the narrow streets. Here, she stood out even more.

"Yes, you want, lady?" said the café employee. His clothing and his unforgiving attitude certainly did not justify the term 'waiter'.

"Coffee, black," she said back in the very same tone. He needed to know she was not intimidated, nor was she 'out of place' here in this exposed square. Soon enough, he returned with a hot cup of coffee.

She sipped her coffee and tried to look uninterested in her surroundings, all the while using her peripheral vision and the reflection from a window to watch the square. She had a good view of almost all the square from where she had chosen to sit. This was not by chance. Nothing was ever left to chance.

After several minutes, a man approached her. She had been aware of the same man standing a distance away, smoking and simply watching. She got ready to stand and strike out if he acted in any way dangerously.

Was he her rendezvous, or was he the lead man in a gang, with others watching and ready to pounce?

"Hey, Jew; you must be the Jewish woman," spoke the man as he closed on her. Shoshanna had turned to face him when he got to within five yards. He continued, "We don't get many white women in this square, Jew, so it is easy for me, no?" The confident smile on his face revealed an arrogant local, safe in his self and happy in his surroundings.

"You're a genius," she replied, as the man pulled out a seat and invited himself to sit at her table.

With men like this, Shoshanna knew it was best to get straight to the point. "What do you have for me?" she asked as she lit her second cigarette. "You know what I asked for and you said you could get it, so you better fucking have them," she concluded, staring him down and watching his hands as he moved. She kept her attention focused on what was going on around and behind her, but for now, she also watched his hands as one entered the bag he had brought.

"The Glock is a very desirable weapon, Jew. People start talking when this gun is the conversation," he said. He kept smiling as he continued. "I had to bullshit a lot of questions when I asked for this piece. So, if you want it, the price has now changed," he said.

"Let me see the piece," she instructed him with a nod, "and slowly."

Pulling the first of two handguns out into the light, her contact knew he had a sale. Shoshanna also knew instantly; it was what she had asked for.

"Christ, you people, how on earth did you get limited-edition G43 fucking 9mm police handguns?" she said with a small laugh. It was hard enough to get such a gun when she served in the military and, yet, this money-motivated thug had two.

"I know the police chief, Jew. He is saving for a new yacht, so, as I said, the price has changed. I need forty thousand Kwanza," he replied, showing her the second handgun, hoping it would help with his request.

"We agreed thirty. Don't fuck with me or I walk," Shoshanna replied in a low voice, her eyes meeting his across the table. She suspected she was not going to have much luck with negotiating this new price down. Both she and her supplier sitting across the table knew her priority was to get the guns, and extract herself safely from her current predicament.

"The chief wanted more, Jew, and I had to pay him. Now, you pay me," he demanded. The man was starting to get nervous and for a reason unknown to Shoshanna, was looking furtively around the square.

Need to act, thought Shoshanna as she wondered what had brought about the subtle change in his demeanour. "Ammunition, how much?"

"Enough," came the sharp reply.

The rendezvous was becoming increasingly uncomfortable for both parties. She sensed he could pull away at any moment. She had to take the risk.

"Done, you fuck." And with that, Shoshanna quickly counted out forty thousand in five hundred bill notes and, as subtly as she could, placed this into a second bag that he had positioned on the table.

"I go first," she said, as she stood and grabbed the first bag from his grip. "I can come back and finish you off, my greedy friend, if I find out you have betrayed me," she said as she glanced around the square and started off.

She could tell from the weight of the bag that there were certainly two handguns and ample ammunition. She just needed to find a suitably hidden area to load one, just in case, it was needed on her exit out of the squalor.

Moving faster and with greater purpose, she felt more secure having a concealed handgun capable of downing a man with ease, should she have any surprise encounters. Choosing a different route from the one that took her to the square, Shoshanna was out and walking the highway that encircled the shanty town in half the time it took her to get there.

He looked the trustworthy type... she thought to herself as a smile flickered across her face. Whether it was relief or just the absurdity of her encounter, she didn't know, but she giggled a little out loud. She had bought illegal weapons from an unknown man, who had done as he was supposed to and not tried to double-cross her. 'Trustworthy', popped back into her head and, again, the smile reappeared.

Having flagged down a taxi and now en route to Tombua, Shoshanna became a little anxious again but for a whole different reason than earlier in the square.

What if it's not as I remember it? She thought. *What if it's not even there – the beach, my beach? Christ, what if I'm doing the wrong thing and I hate being back there?* The thoughts coursed through her brain, round and round. However, for the next two hours, she had no choice but to try and fail, to put such concerns behind her.

The taxi was hot, very hot, but the road outside was dusty, and to open the windows was to invite the drier heat and grit inside. The air conditioning seemed to work when it could be bothered to do so, and both passenger and driver found themselves gravitating towards the air vents on the occasions when it did decide to splutter into action.

Two hours to go. Two hours in a melting pot of a vehicle with polite, albeit perfunctory conversation. It would be a long two hours.

Her beach was on the tip of the peninsula, where the single dirt road giving access seemed to end only because it went directly into the South Atlantic Ocean.

She didn't want the driver to take her straight to her destination, so she racked her brain for a sensible location for him to drop her without arising suspicion. She already knew that a white woman travelling alone here was conspicuous enough. She also pondered whether it was wise to tip the driver enough to persuade him not to tell anyone about his fare, or if tipping would do the opposite, and encourage pirates to come after a seemingly rich and vulnerable white woman. She had time to consider everything as, for now, this dirt road went on for miles.

She also had two powerful handguns and would acquire a hunting knife along the way – a definite mark in her favour.

With the last semblance of civilisation finally approaching, Shoshanna's chance to disguise her end-point from the driver was drawing near. She prepared her bag and the fare, with a modest tip, and instructed the driver where to let her off.

When she got out next to a street café and tiny store on the edge of a village, she stood to watch the taxi disappear back up the road and into the dust, before moving quickly away from the area. It was the hottest part of the day and as such only the goats were exposed to the sun's rays; the few occupants of the village were inside shading from the heat.

Shoshanna couldn't be sure if she had been seen or the taxi heard, but no one had apparently felt it prudent to investigate. She patted one of the two handguns reassuringly as she scaled the first hill that ran parallel to the path. Now, over and out of direct sight, and heading directly on foot to Tombua, her private beach and personal memories were within reach. The thought of going back there was enough to fill her heart with pleasure, mostly. She was indeed beginning to revive her spirit and soul.

Soon, Shoshanna would lose signal on her mobile phone. Soon, she would be out of communication from the world, and very soon, it would be just her and her own thoughts. It was what she craved, but until then, she sat in the shade and pulled out a roughly assembled picnic from her backpack. She needed sustenance for what was ahead. Taking advantage of the remaining cellular coverage, she scrolled her phone for news that might be of interest. She came across one article that caught her attention.

As she scanned the Jewish papers for news of her discovery, she stopped on one article in the *Jerusalem Post*.

A pensioner had been hurt in an unprovoked attack in a suburb of the city. The article detailed how he had suffered severe and possibly crippling leg injuries. He had claimed to the local news channel that it was at the hands of a former female special forces soldier who once lived in the area. It claimed the attack was by Shoshanna Agnon, a young girl who grew up on a neighbouring property and who once was a family friend.

As she pondered the implications of having her name mentioned in the press, Shoshanna decided to carry on, irrespective. The article would be news in that locality, but even if someone was specifically searching for her name online, it was unlikely to lead them to link the dots to any of the other killings. For now, despite a growing sense that the net might be closing, she felt safe enough to continue with her plans.

Shoshanna could not know, she could never have known, that across the ocean, on the East Coast of America, someone was indeed looking for her. Someone had made it their own personal mission to locate and track down Shoshanna Agnon. Shoshanna's initial instinct was right; the net was closing in.

Chapter 13
Beach

Since Shoshanna Agnon had uncharacteristically disappeared from duty, Connor Law had been searching for her. He had not fully believed that such an operator could simply have disappeared whilst on a live assignment. Photographs of her, dead or captured, would be a huge coup for the insurgents and none had surfaced on monitored social media.

The two had conducted operations together a while back and had grown close. Very close. Law was brought into Shayetete 13 to watch, and learn the techniques and ways of this most secretive of units. He impressed command so much that he moved from operational support to 'live' and within a very short while, he was working alongside Shoshanna. The two became close and personnel as a result. As they shared the same commander, they likewise shared the same bed.

Connor had become obsessed with finding her. His feelings for her remained strong. He read the article over and over, trying to determine her next move. What was she doing? Was she hiding something?

Shoshanna always had been a particularly ruthless operator but with a strong moral compass and, if she had stumbled across some injustice, he knew she would have it in her to be the avenger, no matter the targets. Now he knew she was indeed alive, could it really be possible that the deaths of former special forces soldiers were somehow connected to Shoshanna?

Shoshanna walked parallel to the dirt road but far enough away from it to avoid contact, should the odd local cycle past. The road would help her get to her beach; it had been a while since she was last there. The trees had grown and the landscape had likewise altered a little. She didn't yet remember as much as she had hoped. Still, following the dirt road reassured her that she was walking in the right direction.

The heat was taking its toll on her. She was carrying two weeks' worth of supplies and the weapons that she hoped she would not need were also adding to her struggle.

The sun had started to lower in the sky and was readying itself to disappear for the night. Shoshanna used the lengthening shadows to determine how long she had been walking. It was easier to track the sun than to stop and search for her compass, and more importantly, her watch, stuck somewhere in her rucksack.

"Can't be long now. It isn't long now, Sho," she said out loud, reassuring herself that it was indeed not much further before she could offload the weight and relax on the sand. This internal-external dialogue continued back and forth. When she wanted to rest, she would tell herself she was almost there, that the beach was just over the next hill and so, she would not take a break. She would instead carry on toting the weight, getting closer to her goal with every step.

The sun would dip below the undulating terrain a few more times before finally sinking for the evening. Reaching the top of a hill, she looked down and released her grip on the rucksack, sitting down quietly where she had stood. She was back. She was only a few dozen yards from the beach, but had stopped for the first time since exiting the taxi. The smell, the noise of the waves, the overpowering memories had knocked her back and she sat on the hilltop, simply watching the waves attack the sand as they did so relentlessly.

The tide did not retreat and run from her private beach as it did elsewhere. The perpetual noise of the waves meant that with your eyes closed, it was hard to tell if it was day or night. So when Shoshanna awoke, damp from the morning mist, lying on the sand, she was surprised with herself. She had secured the area, hidden the supplies and cleared her tracks, but she was again surprised that she had succumbed to sleep so easily.

Rising up to her feet, still holding the handgun she had clutched throughout the night, she took in her surroundings, searching the sand and shore for anything amiss – footprints or larger animals. All she saw, however, were the tiny trails of crabs, scuttling back into their sand holes as the waves retreated once more.

Her first night back in the tranquil paradise had passed trouble free. She so longed for them all to do the same. She had two weeks of calm and reflection. Time enough to put her world to rights. Two weeks of supplies and two weeks of becoming human again. She looked forward to it.

Shoshanna's first full day of secluded recuperation was spent reworking the wooden hut that she and her former lover had slept in those many years earlier. It had remained in a good state all these years and was made ready with a few easy repairs.

Next on her list of things to do was to seek out the canoe that the two had used to paddle out to sea and catch fish by hanging a baited wire over the edge. She did not expect interference, but she was ever the soldier and the canoe, if it still existed, was a secondary escape route. Right then, however, she had no idea where they had hidden it. Time enough to find it. For now, it was time to cool down in the green water that filled the cove.

Clothes behind on the beach, she dived in naked and swam out a short distance. A handgun was secured in a waterproof bag and tied to a cane pole protruding slightly out of the water. Should she need to, she would not have to come out of the water to protect herself.

The water felt magical. It engulfed her body and mind just as she had remembered. The coolness caressed her figure as he once did when they swam together and laughed for hours. Now it was just her, but that was fine, she told herself.

Shoshanna swam and swam, never losing sight of the cane pole or the beach beyond. This secluded slice of coast had always felt like their private beach and she hoped that the only visitor she might encounter would be the occasional fisherman far out to sea. As she relaxed, her memories came flooding back – mostly happy memories of the time with Connor in their own piece of heaven. Occasionally, she let herself concede to the one memory that she did not want to recall.

The one painful memory was the moment he chose service over love. They had agreed to leave the military together, but when he was asked, he had accepted the return to duty. She was ready then, to leave, but it seemed he was not. She remembered the moment when the helicopter lifted away and he failed to return from the operation, presumed dead. This memory, she feared, would never truly leave her.

Shoshanna swam back and forth along the shore, parallel to her beach, and each time she turned and changed direction, the school of tiny fish that were following her would do the same.

I'm not your fitness instructor, guys, she thought, as she found a weird pleasure from the company.

She was slowly making her way back to shore and her clothes when she remembered where they had left the canoe.

"I'm off, boys, to dig up a canoe," she said to her followers as she reached waist height in the water and stood up.

"Same time tomorrow, team. Don't be late for the class," she called, smiling to herself at the joke as she fixed her eyes on a large piece of driftwood a few hundred yards down the beach.

Dropping the bagged handgun down on the sand, she put her clothes on without pausing to drying her skin. The sun would do that soon enough. Her shirt clung like glue to her torso, hugging the outline of her athletic physique.

Stuffing the weapon down the inside of her cut-off denim shorts, she headed down the beach to the driftwood, which was so obvious from the water and less so, by design, from the beach.

Arriving at the three-meter-long piece of rotting wood, she knew exactly where the canoe was. From the water, the log had a sharp, splintered, arrow-like end, which didn't look like anything unusual from the land. This arrow pointed to one of two sand mounds a further three metres away. Under this hump lay the canoe.

Shoshanna remembered how it had taken them both half a day to dig the hole deep enough to evade shifting sands and bury the canoe. So for now, relaxing as she was, on her secluded beach, Shoshanna decided to leave the retrieval until the next day. Now, she needed food and soon enough, she would start a small fire to cook with.

An hour or so later – for time seemed to stand still – she was filling her stomach with warm food and her mind with more memories.

The light was slowly fading on another day and the flames from the small fire danced around the sand in a joyful manner. Connor had shown her the black ash bush, which was a smokeless burner due to its lack of sap. He had also insisted on specific meal times, when the faint winds blew out to sea. Two concealment measures that she had already been aware of, but she took pleasure in listening to her survival expert instruct as she sat, listened and smiled at him. Shoshanna followed this 'instruction' and would do so every day, handgun by her side, but never expecting or hoping for trouble.

The sun rose the next morning and Shoshanna found herself on the opposite side of the small wooden hut than the one she fell asleep on. "Wow, must have been some real good stuff I was dreaming," she said to herself. "Hope he was good," she quipped as she walked out into the heat of the early morning and started to look around the area for signs of trouble in the night. Again, she found nothing, and again, she was both relieved and unsurprised.

After a tin of canned salmon for her breakfast, she set off to look for something to help her with the dig. She knew she had lapsed, in waiting so long to get her full exit plan into effect, but she felt much less the soldier and more the tourist on her beach. She forgave herself this slip and started out, handgun ever her companion.

With no time-zone difference between England and Angola, Connor Law had risen instinctively at the same time as he always did – as *they* always did. Having flown overnight from Boston to London, he was preparing himself for a further flight, and the overland travel to a private and secluded beach on the coast, near Tombua. Law's body clock might have been on Boston time, but as he boarded the second flight, he would not let that minor detail spoil his travel objective.

Shoshanna had been digging for a couple of hours now and it was hard going. As one makeshift wooden-shovel load was extracted, another would fall back into the hole. The sand was so fine and dry, it was a harder task than she had anticipated and was the reason they had taken so long to bury it initially. Now, working on her own, it was even more demanding.

Perhaps, the ribbing and jokes about his manliness were not justified, she thought to herself as she stood up and rubbed the growing soreness in her lower back.

It would be a little while longer before she could step into the hole. With a combination of lifting and pushing, she finally got the canoe back out onto the surface.

She had collected lots of pieces of driftwood from around the area, and against her better judgement and her former lover's instruction, Shoshanna concealed the hole rather than filled it in. She did not want to have to go through the digging again when she left.

The next hour would be spent covering the sand trail of the canoe, now dragged to the wooden hut, then cleaning it down and checking its water readiness.

The solitary paddle was still in place and overall, the canoe had not taken on any significant damage from its time under the sand.

When Shoshanna cut the rope holding the paddle in place, a wrapped package fell and hit the canoe bottom with a thud.

"No way!" Her eyes opened wide and her mouth gaped in anticipation. "He didn't leave a bottle; he couldn't have…" she said as she unwrapped the familiar-shaped parcel.

"Johnnie Walker Private Label!" she said as she stared at the limited-edition blue bottle in front of her. "Under the bloody sand for years, the fool… we could have had this on our last night."

She allowed herself to imagine him there with her on the beach, the two of them sharing the bottle. But he wasn't there. She came to her senses before the pit of sadness in her stomach became too much to ignore.

"Ok, my lovely new best friend, you are being opened tonight." With a smile, she placed it carefully on a small shelf and prepared to go fishing in the recently recovered canoe.

His plane landed on time at Luanda International Airport and Law spared no time hiring a motorbike. He had a few things to do before heading down a single-lane dirt track towards the coast and this would mean he would have to spend a few days in the capital city.

He would hire a guard, who would double as a guide and make his way into the heart of the shanty town to meet with a man who could provide him a weapon.

First, however, he checked himself into a cheap, discreet hotel, under a false name and using one of many passports his department issued. Now, calling Boston on a secure phone, he coded in and after passing the verbal challenge, was transferred to his section commander.

"Sir."

"So, Connor, is it as hot and run-down as I remember?" came the reply.

"No, chief, there's a shit load of money here. You should see the yachts in the harbour. It's a bloody African Monaco," Law replied. He had been surprised in the changes since his last visit.

"Good for you, then. So, I gave you this trip back in time because I need something from you. I need a man to disappear. Well, the section needs a man to disappear. I will send you the imagery and coordinates. When you have secured them, call me back. We will chat more then," and with that, the conversation abruptly ended.

Law sat on the bed and waited for his smartphone to signal receipt of the encrypted data. When it chirped a few moments later, Law opened the messages, and studied the contents and the image of the man – his target. He did not need to know what this man had done or why; he only needed to acknowledge receipt of the package and call his commander back, which he duly did. The two men would talk for longer this time around.

Yet another day passed by for Shoshanna on her private beach, but as the sun again started to fall into the sea, it would be slightly different from the previous ones. She was indeed relaxing. This little area of private sand was beginning to serve its purpose and relax its only inhabitant, who found such a state of mind very hard to achieve.

Sitting in the canoe, by the edge of the wooden hut and watching the sun fall, Shoshanna held up the bottle of expensive whisky. The blue glass made colourful shards of light as she looked through it towards the orange sun.

Time to toast, she thought to herself as she twisted off the cap.

The sun would disappear and stars would come say hello to her in due course. Shoshanna lay in the canoe now; she still had a good vantage point of the surrounding beach area and her handgun never left her side, but tonight, she lay in the canoe, drinking his whisky of choice, and thought of him.

Shoshanna wondered how he had died. Did he suffer? Did he complete the operation prior? Was he captured? Could he still even be alive? All passed through her mind as the intoxicating effect of the whisky took a welcome hold of her senses. Convincing herself he did not suffer and he was dead, she sat up and prepared to move into the hut for the night. Just before she fell asleep, a new thought passed through her head. *Did anyone else from his unit know what had happened to him? Could I find out?* Then, her relaxed mind took over and forced her to sleep.

The night stars were also out a few hundred kilometres away in the capital city. For now, however, he needed to meet a contact and acquire a weapon. It would be a few days before he would change jobs and head towards a secluded beach.

He had been through the shanty town many times before, but like Shoshanna, he always felt more vulnerable on entry and less so on exit, weapon purchased.

His guide took him to a rundown home and walked back away a short distance as Law went up to the door.

Why the fuck did he do that? Law thought, whilst his senses became fully alert.

He knocked and stood slightly off-centre. He had seen too many knocks responded to with gunshots through the door.

This time, the door was answered by a man who exactly fitted the description given by his section. This slightly eased his misgivings, but he remained alert.

The verbal challenge was exchanged and Law entered. The door closed behind him. When it opened again and he exited with the weapon, he knew more than he had expected.

Connor Law now knew that a white woman, tattooed and athletic, had come to the same contact several days earlier in the market square. He also knew that she had secured two powerful handguns and, although he wasn't told, he instinctively knew where she would be that night. Yet, while it felt obvious to him, it also felt too easy. Was she slipping up, or was she sending him a signal?

The sun rose on the secluded beach, and as usual, Shoshanna was up and checking the snare traps. Her failure to catch any wild hare the previous days had led her to put more traps out. There was only so much tinned food she could stomach. Today, she wanted fresh meat.

Success. One trap held a victim, already garrotted and hanging, almost waiting for her to cook and eat it. As she checked the rest, one further trap yielded results. This time, the hare was hanging and bleeding but not yet dead. As she approached it, instinct took over, and the animal tried in vain and in pain to escape. It failed. She cut the wire and quickly brought its head down hard on a rock. *No pain now, my tasty friend*, she thought as she headed back to the hut, swinging her future meal as she went.

The day panned out as she hoped. She swam, followed again by her small fish friends, her handgun never out of reach. She walked the length of the beach for both security reasons and so she could indulge herself in memories.

Something different was happening on this day, while the sun fell into the sea and Shoshanna drank more whisky. A motorbike engine revved a few hundred kilometres away, with the armed rider making his way towards her. It would take him until the next morning to locate the secluded beach, and even longer for the moment Shoshanna lay in the canoe and drank more whisky, unaware of the force coming towards her.

The national paper would run a story in the morning of the mugging and robbery of the city's mayor, and how it had turned violent, resulting in him being a casualty. He had long been suspected of partnering with the local militia, who wanted to take over the oil reserves and stop Western exploitation of Angola's resources. But, with the mayor now dead and out of the way, Connor Law had kick-started the motorbike engine into life and, smiling at the thought of the headlines, sped off towards the coast.

Law had requested the task in Luganda so he could then take on his conscience and seek her out. He suspected she would have retreated to that beach and the only way to get to her was to be assigned the mayor's assassination. His commander knew this also and while it was never officially sanctioned, Law was given 'holiday leave' to go after her.

When Shoshanna woke suddenly the next morning, it was earlier than usual, even for her. She awoke puzzled by her sweat-covered brow and the rapid beating of her heart. Quickly brushing away the thought that something might be wrong, she slipped into her usual routine.

Handgun by her side, she checked the sand for footprints or signs of anything unusual and the surrounding area for broken branches or disturbed foliage.

Nothing found, as she hoped. Heading for her morning dip, she could still not fully relax. Something needled at her mind and she couldn't figure out what or why.

The swim was uneventful. The group of small fish got their daily exercise, Shoshanna's body was caressed by the warm green waters, and after breakfast, she walked the beach to recover memories and try to be happy in herself.

This morning, she decided to venture farther, and she walked out of sight of the beach and the hut. Taking supplies with her, she sat and watched the horizon as she ate. From her vantage point, she could see ships way out at sea and the end of the land many dozens of kilometres away. It was a reassuring place to be and she promised herself that a stint at this spot should become a daily pilgrimage.

She ate the cooked fish she had caught the day before, together with a tin of mixed vegetables, and stood and stretched. Finishing her meal, she turned, and started to walk down and back to her beach. As she did so, the hairs rose to attention on her neck. Her heart felt like it tried to jump out her chest, hitting her rib cage in the effort.

"Christ, what?" she said out loud. But Shoshanna already suspected…

Returning to her hilltop vantage point, she saw what had bothered her so much.

In the distance and seemingly on its way down the single dirt track towards her, rose the dust trail stirred by a moving vehicle. Again, her training cut in. Checking and analysing the topography, and the anticipated speed of the approaching intruder, she knew exactly what to do next. She knew how much time she had to do it and where to exit from. That said, there was always time for fear and emotion.

"Christ, too far!" she said to herself as she ran towards the hut as best she could. She felt stupid that she had walked so far away from her secluded beach but quickly realised that had she not done so, the vehicle would have been a surprise. At least, she knew about it now – this was one advantage.

As she ran back, she determined the distance and the speed of the intruder, and decided that she had around forty minutes before he would be on top of her. She was expert at such determinations: during her military career, it had often kept her alive as she escaped to the evac point and helicoptered out of danger.

Under an hour to rid the hut of signs of life and get away on the canoe… She knew, however, that hiding her tracks in the sand would be difficult in the short timeframe. She suspected she may have to leave quicker than she would want and could not be certain her departure would be perfectly hidden.

Possessions – all the remaining supplies except survival essentials were now buried in the pre-prepared holes and covered over. Next. Her mind was moving at speed, she had done this sort of evacuation a thousand times before in war zones.

A beach hut would be easy in the time she had. The preparation was already done and she never left anything difficult to clear up, for fear of having to leave in a hurry. This was such a time.

Twenty minutes gone. Perhaps, twenty left until whoever it was would be in contact with her.

The hut was cleaned of all signs of life and Shoshanna dragged the canoe to the water's edge. Throwing in the essential supplies, she went back up and started sweeping the sand with a large branch. Luckily, the wind was blowing, so the man-made marks across the sand would soon look more natural.

Might pull this off, she thought to herself.

One final glance up and down her private beach, and it was into the canoe and out onto the water. Paddle in hand, she started out into the waves and currents, which she knew would take her around the cove and out of sight.

She was around a hundred yards offshore when she turned the canoe and held it in position. She loved her secluded beach. It held so many wonderful memories.

Will I see you again? crossed her mind. Then, "No, damn it, I will see you again!" she said out loud as she started to paddle away at speed.

As she started to turn back out to sea, a glint of light burst into her vision. It came from the beach and more specifically, from one side of the hut, where she kept the canoe at night.

Her mind raced.

Sniper sights? How could he have got here so quickly?

She wondered what else might have caused it.

Stopping once again, she waited for a second glint of light as the canoe bobbed up and down gently on the waves.

A second reflection never came, but she knew something had caused the first. Something she had not seen when she cleaned the area of signs of life?

Paddling out and away towards the currents that would take her to safety, her mind raced, and her heart beat a little faster, but she could not think what might have caused the twinkle.

Then, moments later, Shoshanna's private beach disappeared from view. As it did, she felt a pain in her chest. A sad longing and a fear that her days back in her special place may never happen again. She paddled on a few more kilometres and came ashore, handgun ready.

She need not worry about an ambush on this piece of coastline, which was even more uninhabited and secluded. Rucksack on and handgun secured, Shoshanna pulled the canoe up onto the shore and roughly hid it from sight with branches. She set off on foot. She would return back to civilisation sure enough and the long trek ahead didn't faze her. She was, for the most part, fully charged and fully refreshed.

He was now on the beach. However, there was no emotion when Connor Law returned to the former lovers' secret spot.

Instead, he crawled through the undergrowth, moving with deliberate speed across the sand. His weapon had been waxed to avoid any giveaway of metal and sunlight. Law made his way with ruthless precision towards the wooden hut.

He lay in the sand, concealed from sight, for an hour, just watching. He waited for something to happen, but nothing did. The waves attacked the sand and the gentle wind blew as it always did. But, apart from nature, nothing moved on the secluded beach.

Convinced that she was not in the immediate area, he stood and slowly made his way closer to the edge of the beach. His automatic machine gun was armed and ready. His mind was ready for contact, but as he crashed the hut, there was nothing to meet.

Nothing. No obvious signs of life. A part of him had not really expected any recent signs of activity, but instead, he looked for signs of cleaning and disrupted dust patterns.

Two thoughts fought with each other in his mind. Was he too late; had she gone and simply covered her tracks? Or had she not arrived yet and should he lay a trap? His search of the small hut had not made the answer any clearer.

Then, suddenly, the answer was revealed to him. He had almost missed it. From the corner of his eye, he caught the glint of glass shining from one dark corner. He bent down and brushed away the sand. It was an empty glass bottle and it was his favourite whisky. The glint of light Shoshanna had seen from the canoe, Connor Law now held in his hand.

As he looked out to sea, he knew for definite. Shoshanna Agnon was alive and she had been there. He knew her well. He knew she would come back here and he was right. He also suspected he knew where she would go next.

Law's heart pounded in his chest. It was no longer the adrenaline before a firefight. His heart pounded faster because he suspected that he would see her again. And he didn't know what would happen or how he would feel again when he did.

Chapter 14
Alive

There had been one small piece of the puzzle outstanding for Law. Only two people on the planet knew where the canoe was hidden under the sand. He was one. Now, looking at the hole which once housed the thing, he knew for sure that it was Shoshanna.

He also knew she had gotten lazy. Failing to fill the hole, as well as not conducting a final sweep of the beach, during which she would have likely found and buried the empty bottle, indicated she had lost her edge. She had come to the beach to relax, but Law knew she had slipped up. He also knew that her speedy exit meant that she had spotted him coming. He couldn't be sure if she would know it was him, but he had to assume she did.

Connor Law did know, however, that Shoshanna Agnon was alive after all and not dead in a ditch or buried in a shallow grave, killed by insurgents. As he momentarily enjoyed the surroundings, as he had done many times in the past, he too allowed himself a small glint of a smile.

Three hours had passed since he'd stepped back in time and onto the beach. He had searched for any clues of where Shoshanna would go, or indeed, who she would go after next. He was aware it was giving her time to get away, but he also knew that if he could guess her next move, he could utilise his section's resources and get there before her, or, at least, identify and intercept her next kill.

What he couldn't yet confirm was why she had turned rogue and why she was killing her own. Ever since he had noticed a pattern in the mysterious deaths or disappearances of his special forces brotherhood, he had been determined to find someone to destroy. Betrayal of the SF community by one of its own felt like a vile sacrilege; and now he knew it was her, it felt even worse and more troublesome for him.

Their personal records had led him to one common denominator – Shoshanna had worked with all of them.

A part of him did not want to believe it was her. He wanted to believe that she was simply alive and in hiding, knowing that she had deserted her unit, just wanting a peaceful existence. Then, as he hoped for the good, a wave of reality came over him: Shoshanna was killing her own and she may not have stopped after Kyle Scott in London. He suspected that she had to be stopped and that only he could catch her.

As he considered the pros and cons of searching out the whereabouts of the canoe, Shoshanna was taking her seat on a local bus en route to Luanda, after having paddled and walked over fifty kilometres to civilisation.

The former lovers, now on opposite sides of right and wrong, would again go their separate ways, for the moment.

Shoshanna would board a plane to London and, changing travel modes, get a train north to Inverness in Scotland. Connor Law would take himself back to Boston, and brief the section on his Luanda operation and ask for further time away from main duties. He would ask for a second chance to go after her and, in due course, he would be given his 'downtime'.

"Why, Connor?" asked his section commander.

"She's loose, sir. She's out there, alive and I know where she is going next," he replied, hoping he sounded convincing.

"We need you here, active and on the radar, Connor. Not chasing a former lover with a grudge. Hell, who knows what you would do when you caught up with her. Your files show that you were ready to leave Shayetet with her and hang up your boots. How do I know you wouldn't do that again?"

"Sir, if I want to hang up my boots, that decision is mine to make, sir, with respect, not yours," he replied, but sensing there was more to come, he was allowed the remark without response by his commander.

Law lifted his gaze from the table and stared at Commander Richardson directly.

"Sir, David Spencer was assassinated using bitrixomal 377. Only we use that. Kyle Scott was finished off in the same way in London. He was responsible for the op that went bad with her.

Ridge left her for dead and now he's disappeared filming a fucking survival programme. Shall I continue?" said Law, he was aware he was coming across as arrogant, yet, he couldn't conceal his frustration.

Richardson let him vent his anger, saying nothing back.

"I hear on the black vine that Vitschencko was killed in an illegal fight. He worked with her on the Chernobyl mission. You know, the one which resulted in several school kids burning to death."

Richardson interrupted the one-way conversation.

"What's that got to do with us?"

"He was killed in a cage fight…" there was a pause, then came the punch, "by a *woman*."

Then, "Remember Marte?" and as Law was about to explain the connection, Richardson interrupted again.

"Yes, I know, I know. Killed on a British destroyer by a woman impersonating an officer. Ok, wait…"

A few seconds passed and both men reflected on what was said between them.

Richardson stood and walked to the window. Now with his back to Law, he sighed deeply, then spoke again.

"Where next?"

"Scotland," Law replied, daring to hope that Richardson was finally on his side.

"Who?"

"It's one of us."

Richardson turned to look at Law. Law started to say something, but Richardson lifted a hand to gesture for Law not to continue. He had already figured it out and spoke first.

"It's Torah. She's going after Torah, isn't she?" he asked.

"Sir, yes, I believe so."

"We think she will return to London now and possibly contact her female friend again, some journalist, before going north. We have the woman's phone tapped and she has a watcher," he said confidently.

Now certain he could persuade his senior officer to let him take on this mission, Law laid bare his newly thought out plan: "I can get to him before she does. Give me two weeks. She knows he will have protection, so she will have to plan." With that, Law stood and waited.

"Right. You have your two weeks," Richardson said, after a short period of reflection. "Listen, you are taking support…"

"Sir, I am better on my own, you know this!" barked Law back at his commander.

"She will figure out it was you at the beach soon enough. She knows how you operate as much as you her. You're taking Sarah Philips from Section 2 and Jenner. You know Jenner. That's the condition," he said as he walked towards his protégé, Connor Law.

"Sir, Philips and Jenner. Ok, sir. Right, sir," said Law, accepting that he had no alternative but to accept his commander's direct order.

Law continued, "Shall I alert Torah, sir, and tell him…" Again, he was interrupted.

"No, do not contact him. She will know we are on to her if she sees anything other than usual security," Richardson said in a firm voice.

"Yes, sir, of course, sir," Connor Law said, before turning and leaving the office.

On a vast estate thirty miles north of the Scottish town of Inverness, Abel Torah sat and ate dinner with his wife. His children had long left home. His three security guards often ate with them, given the remoteness of their location and the dullness of their routine assignment. Not much happened on this quiet estate except the occasional flurry after a bird shoot or a visit from a passing deerstalker.

Abel Torah was Shoshanna Agnon's former Shayetet 13 commander. Now she was coming after him.

Chapter 15
North

At three London InterCity rail stations, three women prepared to board their trains. All were heading north.

Meanwhile, every major London station was watched by assets from Connor Law's section. They watched for her. They had been briefed on both her physical appearance and her ability to slip past. She was a master at circumventing security and this had kept Shoshanna alive many times on operations around the world.

As the women readied themselves for their journey, Shoshanna waited.

All wore sunglasses, summer hats and casual clothing, and none hung around the station foyer. As instructed and paid, they went directly onto their respective trains.

All three women had been carefully selected for their enthusiasm and also their ability to follow simple instruction. All three had been paid very well. Shoshanna had found single mothers relying on government pay-outs easy targets for the lure of money, travel and shopping. How they secured their dependents that day, Shoshanna did not care.

Now on board their trains and all departing at similar times to each other, they looked forward to their free day out, in three different cities along different routes, destination Northern England.

Shoshanna had provided each woman with a 'pay as you go' mobile, and a poorly disguised script as to what they were up to and where they were going. Each woman had likely experienced the pain of a cheating or violent partner and Shoshanna had played on this. She had told them that she was being followed by a violent husband and that she needed to get away to have safe time with her child. Each understood Shoshanna's feigned predicament and each was happy to help this stranger. The large sum of money didn't hurt.

Between 11.00 and 11.23, the three trains pulled out of three different stations in London and started their respective journeys north.

"Commander, the assets have confirmed Agnon on the train…" said Law, over the phone. "But, we have a major problem, sir," he followed, in a more humble voice.

"Yes, and the problem is?" the commander referred back to Law.

"There are three of them."

There was a moment's silence as the commander tried to make sense of the situation. Law explained further, feeling rather foolish: "Sir, three assets have coded-in with confirmed sightings of our target at three different stations, getting on three different trains… sir," Law said, fully expecting an angry retort.

Sure enough, it came as anticipated.

"Three bloody Shoshanna Agnon's, Law? Christ, you lost one previously and now you're telling me we have three? Explain yourself!" Richardson demanded, with clear exasperation.

"Sir, she knows we're on to her and that we would be watching the stations. I am sure two are decoys. She knows the section's resources are stretched and I think she's made her second mistake," replied Law, trying to sound confident.

Connor was frustrated. He was frustrated with his failure to anticipate the diversionary tactics of Shoshanna – he should have anticipated this. He was more frustrated that their showdown may now not be happening anytime soon. He needed to know how he felt about her. For that, he had to face her up.

"Connor," came straight back from Richardson, now is a more controlled manner, "we both know that our operators don't make mistakes. Everything is a signal. So why should I believe you now?"

Another moment's silence felt like an eternity to Law.

"Sir, the bottle on the beach, not filling the hole with the canoe, sir, she's losing it. I think this is another. She's gambling on us being stretched and that we don't take on all three trains. Sir, we need to act, sir, I need grab teams now!"

Defiant and confident again, Connor Law waited for the phone to spark back into life with the answer and, he hoped, the authority to act as he felt was needed.

"Right, Connor, I let you go after her once, yet, you lost her in Angola. Last time I looked, this section was not a personal vendetta agency," Richardson barked. Connor knew there was more to come. He knew his commander, but he already knew he was getting one last chance.

"I will give you ten days to sort this. You have clearance to *Adonai*."

He had just been given Israel's highest level of security clearance and he knew he now had what he needed to complete the task. Nothing could be kept from him anymore.

"Use the resources wisely and don't fail, Connor. I will be watching you. Philips from Section 2 will report to me direct. Do what you must, but do one thing..." and again the conversation went quiet.

"Sir?"

"End this once and for all, Connor," came loudly down the line before the call ended sharply.

Connor knew exactly what to do next.

Walking quickly into the operations room, he sat next to the analyst whom he trusted most.

"Sarah, I have clearance now to run this the way I want," he said, already starting to figure out his plan in his head.

"Yes, Connor, but you know I have to see the authentication, its procedure," she replied, unwilling to action any request without visual confirmation prior.

"Sarah, it's time-critical, I have it. Let's get going," he snapped back. But he knew she was right. He knew she would not budge on her procedures or relationships. It was, after all, why he trusted her most.

"Right, I will get you 'Adonai', but can you do one thing now?" he questioned softly. Sarah smiled in acceptance.

"I need snatch teams at these locations in under an hour," he said, as he handed her a piece of paper with the names of three English cities along the routes of the trains. "Can you activate them now at least?"

Again, Sarah smiled back at Connor. "Get visual," she said, as she turned to her screen and, picking up the secure line, started dialling a number that would activate 'sleepers' throughout Northern England.

On three separate trains, now moving at speed towards three different Northern cities, three women sat, and read and drank coffee. Each was unaware of their pending future at the first station and each was satisfied that they were doing the right thing by assisting a woman in a violent relationship.

At the same time, under a railway arch in a lock-up garage, a motorbike fired up. Its exhaust bellowed out the noise of its powerful engine to anyone in earshot. As the rider and bike left the arch, and turned left towards the motorway, the lock up would be abandoned and exposed. Officially surplus to requirements, there was no longer a need to 'lock up'.

Shoshanna powered the bike up through the gears in and out of traffic. She was indeed going north, but she was not yet going after Torah. Instead, she was heading for a rundown council estate on the edge of Manchester. Specifically, a small semi-detached house in a cul de sac in the estate where grieving parents sat and held the picture of their dead son. He was their pride and joy, and they remembered the day he told them he had joined the Royal Navy and that his first posting was on board a British destroyer, called HMS *Dragon*.

Shoshanna was on her way to pay them a visit but not in a manner that they should fear. Her heart held less hatred these days. Instead, she had a Judas gift for the grieving parents.

Not only was she beginning to feel emotions of guilt, but she also knew that when her gift was delivered it would give away her location to pursuers. She didn't care; she had her objective in Manchester and set off at pace to get there.

The next thirty minutes would be annoyingly uneventful for Law. He would pace the operations room, and watch the many monitors pushing out data and images. He would glance at the clocks on the monitors that counted down to when each train would arrive at its first scheduled stop.

The snatch teams were in place, waiting, and briefed about exactly who they were after and how dangerous she was. They were told that she would most likely be expecting something to happen. They were told they had last-resort clearance to use weapons on a foreign national's train and risk collateral damage. The section would manage the mess after, should it come to it.

The three snatch teams waited discreetly, mingling with the other passengers standing on the platform waiting for their train north.

The operations room went quiet as the first train slowed as it reached the platform. They had taken over control of the station's CCTV cameras, and, together with body-worn cameras, Connor could see and hear live feed as they entered the train. The earlier passenger check had taken First Class out of the equation, so they had less carriages to run.

When it stopped and the automatic doors unlocked, they went in at the designated point, and separating left and right, pushed past passengers and luggage as they sought their target. They had done this sort of thing thousands of times before, and while this rendition was not in any way legal, the British and Israeli Governments had an understanding.

Law saw two operatives stop at one seat, and seemingly fall over a woman wearing a summer hat and dress. What they never saw was the syringe enter her neck and the disabling effect the contents had.

The first two operatives were rapidly joined by the other two and within ninety seconds, the first of the three decoys was off the train and heading towards the back of a black van, and a very hard and long interrogation.

There was a real sense of relief around the operations room when the first snatch team coded-in with the confirmation that their target was acquired.

Then, a few minutes later, the second train pulled into its scheduled stop.

The process was repeated. The search, the pushing, the obvious fear felt by passengers as they witnessed a woman being rapidly dragged out of her seat by a group whose faces were masked. Second snatch team coded-in. One to go.

Connor watched the screens and pondered. The first two went very well, too well. He knew the odds that the third and last grab could be her, so for the time being, he stayed focused and on plan.

When the third snatch team coded-in, there was a noticeable exhalation of relief around the room from the analysts and support staff.

"Shit, we don't have her!" seethed Law as he started thinking what he missed. "It was too easy; she's not there and she wasn't on the fucking trains! She would have put up a fight or worse. They were decoys, all three were fucking decoys! Shit, she's not on any bloody train!" It was a fierce diatribe, but really aimed at himself and his own frustrations.

He waited a few minutes more for the images of the three women to be transmitted over the secure comms and when they arrived, he saw what he already knew. He walked towards the door of the operations room both frustrated and angry. They had the wrong woman, three wrong women and there would now be a political mess to clear up. He stopped and turned back to the analysts, all now quiet after his outburst, awaiting further instruction.

Law spoke, "Go back to CCTV of the three embarkation stations. Review the passengers who boarded the very next trains after the decoys. She may have sent them on as sitting ducks and sneaked aboard after the confusion." He knew she would not have, but he also felt he needed to say something to try to stay in control of the situation. Then, from one corner of the room, an analyst shouted out.

"Sir, social media is starting to trend…" but she was swiftly interrupted by a still-angry Connor Law.

"Yes, I know, the wrong woman being dragged off a fucking train," he snapped, slamming the door behind him as he stepped out for some air. He would have some difficult conversations with his commander and the British Secret Service equivalent, and he needed to cool off.

Around an hour after the operations room in London went quiet, contemplating their failure, Shoshanna was arriving in Manchester. Following the road signs and her phone's sat nav, she arrived at the council estate and parked her bike. She would be free to walk the pavements without her helmet on as she was not expected or known there.

A few discreet chats to shop owners and elderly residents later, and she had narrowed down the address to two houses in a cul de sac on the west side of the estate. There was a play park behind and a small wooded area beyond that. She reviewed her surroundings, determining an escape route should it be needed. Then she sat out of direct line of sight of both houses and waited. It would not be too long before she had the confirmation she needed.

A family friend of the parents always confirmed the loss of their beloved son when asked. She knew they would. At times of sadness, people need to share their grief, and a simple 'you look down' resulted in all the detail and confirmation Shoshanna needed to determine which of the two houses she would visit that night.

Returning to her bike and checking the route for security cameras, she rode off towards a garage to fill up on petrol and grab some food. She would return on foot later, when the sun had set.

Like with most cities, the pollution and glow from the street lights hid the stars in the sky. So when Shoshanna walked out of the woods and scaled the small wooden fence of the play park, she was already well hidden from sight. She was well versed at moving without being seen, so this entry would be an easy one. It would also be an emotional one, unexpectedly. She was growing a conscience and she didn't yet know how she felt about that.

With the back door lock dealt with in under three seconds, Shoshanna was in. Walking first into the kitchen, she stood and listened to the house noises. Was there anything unusual? She didn't see a dog earlier that day, but now, she scanned the kitchen for signs that the parents had pets. *Nothing*, she thought.

Now, into the living room and then, as the moonlight continued to power her night-vision goggles, she saw the first of many pictures that confirmed she was in his parents' house.

Shoshanna picked the first photo up from above the fireplace. She raised her night goggles and, with a torch, illuminated the photo. Straight away, she recognised the same young sailor who had been courteous and allowed her to pass first under the hatch one floor down on HMS *Dragon*. She remembered his smile and his 'Ma'am' as he signalled that she pass before him.

She replaced the photograph exactly where she had found it. Her heart beat a little faster now, but it was not because of any fear of detection. There was some new emotion that she felt more and more – guilt.

Shoshanna looked around the room. The streetlight cast an orange glow through the cheap curtains so she could see well enough without her night-vision aid. She looked for the best location to leave the envelope.

Settling on a second picture of the son, she lifted it from the wall where it hung and placed it upright against a vase on the table. She then left the envelope leaning against the photograph. Lastly, pulling a small item from her chest pocket, she placed it next to the envelope bulging with money and quietly left the house the way she had entered, disappearing back into the copse behind the small playground.

Hours after the sound of a motorbike starting up and disappearing in the distance, the dead sailor's parents would wake and come downstairs.

What they saw would initially scare them, confuse them. The photograph of their son's naval graduation had been taken off the wall and was now accompanying an envelope that they would later determine had ten thousand pounds in it. Stranger than that, a small plastic dragon sat pride of place next to the picture.

The police and forensic teams would scan the house for clues but none would be found. The neighbourhood CCTV would likewise show nothing. However, when the local newspaper reported the occurrence and ran a photograph of the small dragon, analysts hidden at an undisclosed address in a secure building would pick up on the story and transmit the detail to Connor Law.

He knew who had visited the elderly parents and he now knew why. The last piece of the puzzle had truly fallen into place. The difference between current and earlier 'mistakes' made by his foe was that he knew she no longer cared. He knew there was no mistake at the house and that she was, in fact, sending him a signal. 'Catch me if you can'.

Chapter 16
Waiting

There was a flurry of activity in Connor Law's section offices. Richardson had drawn in additional support and logistics, and the team hunting Shoshanna had grown to over twenty. Each analyst tapped away on their computer or moved maps and charts around their desk.

Connor would spend time in and out of the secure offices, and each time he left, with the team turning up no new leads, he would get more and more frustrated.

"I don't need this wait, sir," he said to his commander. "I should be going north with Philips and Jenner. Let me just get on with it, sir," he barked, clearly annoyed at what he thought was a lack of activity, which was playing straight into her hands.

"Listen, you rushed in before and while I agree it may give Agnon more time to plan, it also gives you the time you need to do it right this time," Richardson responded firmly. "You're staying here until we capture her movements and her route. I have given you this last chance and I'm not allowing you to fuck it up by diving in."

Law would, soon enough, head back to his flat for the night but not before calling into the watcher placed on Shoshanna's only confirmed friend, Lisa. This would also result in nothing valuable.

Clutching at straws, he thought to himself as he walked home. *It's what we're trained to do, so why on earth am I surprised? And why so bloody angry?* He questioned himself as he entered the underground station, quickly moving down the escalator and boarding a waiting train to Canary Wharf.

Pressing the lift button, he made his way up to the top floor flat used by the section to monitor the comings and goings of the board of global banks, before passing details to watchers on street level. It was commonplace for allies to spy on each other.

This assignment, however, was not about spying. It was of hunting and killing, and to date, there was none of either going on – not on his side, anyway.

It was a time for waiting. Everyone was waiting, but on either side of the equation, they didn't realise the enemy was too.

Connor Law sat and waited in his assigned flat high above Canary Wharf, and looked out over the canals and the tall buildings. He had a panoramic view of London, but at this moment, as he looked out across the rooftops, he saw nothing. His head was filled with operational matters and they did not allow him the luxury of insignificant visualisation.

His commander, Richardson, waited in his offices, reading classified papers and planning assignments for personnel other than Connor Law. He was running several operations concurrently and Shoshanna Agnon was just one of them – the one that was potentially the most messy, but still just one of several.

Lisa sat in her small London flat in the peace and quiet of the aftermath of her two children's bedtime, and thought about her life and its direction. Occasionally, this would include thoughts of Shoshanna. She made herself a cup of tea and sat quietly, enjoying the calm and wondering whether she might read or watch a film.

The section team assigned to tracking Shoshanna ran the diagnostics and viewed hour after hour of motorway CCTV, airport security-camera footage and train-station foot-passengers. But they too waited. They waited for that lucky break that would tell them where she was and what route she was taking north towards her ultimate target, Torah.

Then there was Shoshanna. She leaned against her motorbike in an unlit part of a service station some way up the west coast, eating a tasteless motorway sandwich and thinking. She was thinking about her final assignment as well as Connor Law. She had determined that he was her pursuer in Angola. Her instinct told her and it was rarely wrong. Shoshanna also waited but, as she did so, she planned and thought.

Perhaps, I have two final targets, she considered carefully. Her heart pounded faster inside her biker leathers. Could she kill her former lover? After all, she suspected he had come after her

148

to do the same. It was just that a part of her still wondered if there were feelings for each other.

Now rested, the burst of engine activity as she started the bike brought her back to the present. She sped away, and headed for the motorway and towards the Scottish Border. She couldn't have known that a small security camera at the rear exit of the petrol station had recorded her image through the darkness. Careful as she had been to scope out all surveillance, she was not – as she was beginning to realise – completely infallible. Law's team back in London also didn't know that they had their first real lead, but they had less than twenty-four hours to discover it. Otherwise, the camera unit would record over it the next day. The clock was ticking.

By the time the evening team conducted the hand-over to the new crew, Law had already been wading through the security-camera footage and live feeds for over two hours. Necking his fourth coffee, he gave the new crew a nod of acknowledgement then returned to the screens of people and vehicles scurrying around in all directions trying to get to their destinations by the shortest available route.

Shortest available route, he thought. *She won't go by the shortest available route*. Then, as he started to figure it out in his head, words came out of his mouth. "She will go the longest way, the least obvious way…" His voice caught the attention of two analysts preparing to take their own places at the monitors.

Law continued speaking out loud, to himself mainly. He needed the reassurance that he was not going to miss her and let her go again.

"So she will get away from the cameras and not be noticed. No speeding, no obvious cars. What else?" There was an awkward pause as the two analysts looked at each other and wondered to themselves if this was a question they should try to reply to.

"How can she hide in plain sight? How can she get north and be seen by us but not seen by us?" Turning to his two puzzled team members, he spoke again.

"So, she won't go on public transport. Too many cameras and she knows we are watching them. She won't do plane, nor likely drive – security at airports and motorway cameras and registration checks. She will know we will monitor cars reported stolen and rental companies have been informed what to look for. So, how will she get to him?" he said, but he already knew how.

Then, before either of the analysts could deduce her travel mode, Law told them.

"She's hiding from us in plain bloody sight. Bike and helmet; it's obvious now," he said with a grimace, a little frustrated that this epiphany had not arrived with him sooner.

Catching up with their section leader, one analyst spoke.

"And we know she was in Manchester yesterday – so we check motorbikes from the west heading north. Then…" but he was abruptly stopped by Law.

"Too many. Impossible. And helmets obscure faces. Christ, think!" Law sharply interrupted through gritted teeth.

"Petrol," said the other analyst, hoping to justify her position on the team. "Bikes need petrol. We don't check motorbikes. We check petrol stations. They have CCTV. Even Agnon needs petrol and helmets have to be taken off for security, don't they?"

"Yes, right. Grab the feeds from the last twelve hours inside and out of all the stations on her route." As Law paused, both analysts smiled at their discovery, hoping for an acknowledgment from their new boss. But Law was not the smiling type. "I want payment-desk and pumps footage reviewed. Now! What are you waiting for?" With the sharpness of his order ringing in their ears, they both turned and feverishly tapped away at their computers.

Law stood up and walked to the front of op centre. Standing in front of the large wall of monitors buzzing live feeds from locations around the North of England, he caught the room's attention.

"Right, she's travelling on a motorbike, or yesterday she was. We know she's north or east of Manchester and we know she's heading towards *him*. Forget the obvious. She won't do obvious – think outside the box, team, and do it quickly." Law strode to the exit and out towards Richardson's office along the corridor.

Meanwhile, as Law updated his section commander on progress to date, Shoshanna had stopped again. This time, she parked up in a trucker's café and entered the building. Confident that no security cameras were located in or around the stop, she took her helmet off and unzipped her leathers. Now out of the

150

heavily padded gear, as a lone female biker with a statuesque, athletic figure, she had made quite a noticeable entrance.

The long distance lorry drivers would usually only have their imagination to entertain them hour after hour and yet, here, in this partly run-down café, they couldn't help but stare at this vision in front of them.

Shoshanna smiled to herself. *Sad lot*, she thought, but weirdly appreciated that she would have also stared, had this happened in front of her too.

Sitting down in a booth, she picked up the menu and pretended to read it. She was, however, gauging the level of interest and locating the exits, should she need them. Her instincts had again taken over and once satisfied that she was, as she thought, in no danger, she properly turned her attention to the menu.

She ordered something light to eat and started putting the next part of her travel plan into place. Her actions needed to be much more measured; for they were on to her. She had to be the ultimate covert warrior now.

As Shoshanna sat and ate, considering which of the several lorry drivers to approach, a few hundred miles away in London, Connor Law's team made the breakthrough they desperately needed. They had their first sighting of her and at last, had their confirmation.

"I have her," said a member of the team, sitting quietly in front of a grainy image on a screen. "I have her!" her voice rose with certainty as a tangible charge lit the atmosphere in the stuffy room. Like everyone on the case, Smith had been desperate to be the one who unearthed that crucial piece of information and she positively glowed with pride at her discovery.

"She was at this service station last night, sir," said Smith as Connor leant over the desk behind her, eagerly surveying the footage. "I've used enhancement software to confirm. It's definitely her." With Law pulling up a swivel chair and leaning in further, Smith continued, "There, in the gloom, at what appears to be the rear elevation of the service station, a woman, on a motorbike… clearly trying to stay hidden and undetectable."

"Good, show me again," said Law. "How did we get these images?"

As the undisputable picture of his former lover and their prey, appeared large on the central monitor, Smith began to explain where the footage had come from.

He would not fully hear her reply, nor would he actually care. Shoshanna, it seemed, had made a real mistake. Law stared and thought for a moment, lost in his past, yet, planning the future.

As he watched the clip repeatedly, it became clear that Shoshanna had missed a small rear-exit security camera. Connor was filled with conflicting emotions, his eyes transfixed on the image of a face he had not seen in a very long time. A face that had narrowly escaped him in Angola. One that had shared his bed in the past, and now one that he must find and take down. Once and for all.

The waiting was over.

They had what they needed.

They had an up-to-date image of their target.

Connor instructed the team to run the software algorithms on the face on the screen and send it back through the CCTV footage to look for further matches. Then, before leaving the op centre, he turned and pulled up a chair. Something had been bothering him.

He spoke directly to one of the team, "The SEAL, Spencer, the assassination a few months back? There was a woman, I seem to remember… caught on CCTV but not clear and they couldn't identify her. Do me a favour. Run the software on that image and tell me if it could have been Agnon." He stood and left. He already felt he knew the answer but procedure had to be followed.

Returning to the section apartment he was borrowing, high up in in Canary Wharf, Connor sat with a scotch and thought about the day.

Why did she go after Spencer? What did he do that made her go all that way to take him out? Then there was Ridge. *What's joining the dots?* He pondered and drank for a while longer. Frustrated that he was clearly missing something, he stood and walked towards the bank of floor-to-ceiling windows, staring at his reflection mirrored eerily in the darkness outside. He should have it solved by now.

Vitschencko the Russian and Agnon… Bohdan, he was likely the facilitator. Find Bohdan. With that thought, he coded-in to the operations room.

The call was answered swiftly. "Sergi Bohdan. Find Bohdan, and ask him about the Russian and Agnon. We're missing something. Perhaps, he can give us what we need," he said, before slamming the phone down on the desk. The alcohol and his emotions were beginning to fight each other.

Moments later, against his better judgment, Law made another phone call.

The recipient's mobile rang and rang. No one answered and there was no voicemail option. He ended the call and poured himself yet another scotch.

Meanwhile, in a remote estate in Northern Scotland, Abel Torah looked at the screen of his mobile. It showed a missed call from Connor Law. He too sat and after a moment's reflection, called in his two bodyguards. They would be told that the game had changed. That he had been compromised and to prepare themselves.

Before falling asleep in his chair, now worse for wear from too much whisky, Law decided he was going to make his second deliberate mistake in the morning. He would confront Richardson and get answers to why Shoshanna was after Torah. Somebody knew something and they weren't telling him.

As his eyes closed for the night, his mind slept. He would wake the next day still determined to confront his section commander, but this morning, he would not be in quite as early. He needed the alcohol demons left in his head to depart first.

When Law eventually wandered into the operations room, still feeling weary after his night of drinking, his team had made progress on his earlier demand.

Sergi Bohdan had been found. He had been found dead in his bed, shot through the head. Lying next to him were two prostitutes, who had also been shot. Bohdan had been tracked down by the fight organiser, who had lost over a hundred thousand dollars when Shoshanna killed Vitschencko. That lead was now formally cold.

Richardson had been expecting Law. He finally agreed to speak with him. Making him wait for over an hour had been deliberate. Richardson needed to determine what Torah would do next. Late the previous night, he had received a text message from his former chief informing him of Connor Law's contact and Richardson needed to know what action Torah would take, so he could play his cards appropriately.

Torah would stay put.

He would strengthen the defences but would stay where he was. He knew well what was developing – what was coming for him. He suspected that Connor Law would be making his way towards him too, into his life again. He also suspected he knew why this place, at this time. He would stay put, but he would prepare the area for new arrivals.

So Richardson would send Law up north with the two others assigned to him and, the next day, the team would monitor Shoshanna Agnon's progress, trying to establish exactly how and when she planned to attack.

"Sir, I want to get straight to the point," said a clearly agitated Connor Law.

"Well, that would be good," replied Richardson without turning to face his colleague.

"Are you telling me everything you know about Agnon, sir? Are you protecting her, or worse, are you protecting me, sir?" asked Law, his head beginning to pound. He had his suspicions but he was still confused. "You see, sir, it's just that she was easily tracked before. The earlier killings – you could have tracked her and snatched her a while back if you had wanted to. So again, sir, is there something I need to know?"

There was a difficult silence, but again, it was Connor Law who first broke it. Now in a more thoughtful and considered manner, he spoke to his line manager and, strangely, to himself as he tried to work through what was confusing him.

"So, say she was present at all the incidents and killings that she blamed on her targets, then, perhaps, she saw more than what we know? Perhaps, Agnon saw something that you are using elsewhere. It's why you're keeping her alive."

Richardson turned to face Law.

"I am not keeping her alive. I sent you after her, didn't I?" Again, there was silence. Richardson moved towards his desk and stood by his chair.

"I am doing so again. You have tonight to prepare. At sunrise, you fly north to Scotland," he ordered. Then, moving his seat to allow him to sit, Richardson waved Law off and out of his office. He then sat down and picking up the telephone receiver, started to dial out.

The waiting was nearly over for everyone in this most dangerous puzzle.

While the killing party of three boarded the unmarked private jet out of London City Airport, destination a private airstrip a few hundred miles north, near Inverness, Shoshanna Agnon was waking in her temporary accommodation a few miles from her prey. She did not feel different or have a change of plan. Instead, knowing this could be the day she saw the only two men from her past who could rival the admiration of her father, she sat up and prepared some breakfast.

Chapter 17
Watching

It was happening more and more in the last few weeks. Shoshanna would toss and turn throughout the night, demons dancing around in her subconscious, only to wake early in the morning with a headache.

This morning was no different. Taking pills to try to calm the pounding going on in her head, she walked into the shower. Naked and with the water on cold, she stepped in. The fresh chill made her flinch and exhale sharply. However, it was the best remedy for her aching brain, clearing it of the many fuzzy images that forced their way into her mind's eye. It did not, however, have the cleansing effect that the shock of cold water usually did. She was growing more accustomed and it was wrong.

She had a sense that she was denying something but could not yet determine what it was. She knew she was hiding from herself and a truth that she didn't want to confront yet. The thumping in her head and the images running wild across her imagination made the start of each morning something she dreaded. The cold water seemed to cool her thoughts and bring her momentary relief.

Shoshanna stood under the shower, her body soaked in cold running water. She did not allow herself to accept the cold, nor the involuntary reaction to shake or step out. Shoshanna forced her body to stay. She had to get out but never truly wanted to. She enjoyed the calm and the cold but she had to make her way onto the estate later, and start to formulate a plan for Torah.

She suspected that Connor Law, and no doubt others, would soon be close and out to stop her. They may already be close, but for now, she turned the shower off, and allowed the water to drain and her body temperature to slowly rise again.

Twenty minutes later, she was stepping out of the room, out into the street and into obscurity. She had hidden the motorbike and her leathers, and was now submerged in the world of those around her. Her warm, thick clothing and hiking boots meant Shoshanna could walk amongst people without too much concern of being spotted or standing out. She hid her swagger and her tattoos, but if they were to see the fire in her eyes, then and only then would they see a woman who others needed to be worried about – especially those in law enforcement.

In front of her, reaching high above the roofs of the street buildings, Ord Hill rose on the shore of the Moray Firth. Her first task for the day – to walk to its summit, and from there find a secure location from which she could monitor the activity in and around the estate that housed her target.

With a fully stocked rucksack on her back, she looked like any other mountain walker. For the first part of the climb, Shoshanna kept to the well-trodden footpaths, trying not to appear anything other than a tourist to the many true walkers following along or down the same footpath, having conquered their own personal quests. Apart from the occasional polite acknowledgement, she kept her head down, and avoided any conversation by simply walking the path and heading slowly upwards towards the summit in front of her.

Section 2 was the logistical arm of Richardson's covert department and in Sarah Philips, Law had the best resource and hardest working analytical mind he could hope for. By the time the private jet landed and the cabin door had opened, Philips's requests were laid out in 'rhino' boxes just inside the hanger in front of the now stationary jet. Inside each of the three armoured boxes was an array of weaponry and equipment that would make the most battle-hardened soldier light up with excitement. She had requisitioned items from the armoury and these had arrived ahead of the three designated assassins now walking towards the waiting car. The support staff would load the boxes onto a following jeep, and together, Law, Philips and Jenner would make their way to their temporary accommodation, less than two miles from where Abel Torah slept at nights with his family.

Now, there were six against Agnon, ready to face her down in any firefight she chose to initiate. Six was a small number for her. She may not have fully known how many there were, but if she had, she would have accepted and smiled that they were so few.

Law chose the hut closest to the entrance of the estate, while the other two had similar huts separated by a small stone wall but also not too far from the entrance. Protocol determined that they had separate secure sleeping accommodation in order to avoid a wipe-out attack from a hostile.

They secured their equipment, and would meet a short while later for a debrief and secure sat phone link with operations in London. Any new details relating to their target since the flight north would be welcomed.

Shoshanna also had an array of equipment that would support her in the field and when she found a secure watching point, she went about making it suitable and ready for the many hours she anticipated spending there.

It had taken Shoshanna just over four hours to reach the summit and part-scale part-crawl her way some distance down the other side towards a series of depressions in the grass which, covered with heather and shrubs, would prove innocuous and perfect for her task. Around seven hundred metres from the first outbuilding, where his bodyguards lived, her high-magnification binoculars and night-vision goggles would easily pick up on activity.

She could see the smoke rising from the larger of the two buildings further inside the secure perimeter fence, in which Shoshanna knew Abel Torah lived. The smaller building appeared currently unoccupied, probably as the bodyguards were on shift and with the family or with Torah himself. Waiting and watching would soon provide answers to the many questions in her head.

So it was, on this private deer estate high in the Scottish mountains, three separate groups waited and watched. One monitored activity of a family and their bodyguards. One watched out for signs of someone observing the family, who themselves simply waited, knowing they were under scrutiny.

Jenner and Phillips would walk the estate together, looking like hikers. Unfamiliar to Shoshanna or Torah's men, they could hide in plain sight. They would periodically call in to Law, who preferred to move covertly across the hillside. He would take hours to move a few hundred yards. He knew how she operated because he knew how to do so himself. He looked for a solid vantage point at all times. If he could find a spot where he would be comfortable to hold down, then he felt he would also find her there.

They operated like ghosts, but for Agnon and Law, they were twins. Find one by already knowing the other's exact modus operandi…

The next day started like the one before. Shoshanna Agnon would prepare a calorie-dense cold meal to fill her stomach before doing what little stretching and relaxing she could in her spot. This would be her only exercise for a while, as she settled down again to monitor, and record the comings and goings from the stone houses in her sights. Still no sighting of Torah but she had carefully followed the routine and timing of his two bodyguards' perimeter searches.

The three assassins sent north from London would separate and mingle with locals in the nearby town, trying to glean any information relating to the sighting of a woman with an out-of-place accent. Law would plan his search route and timings for the day, while Torah would sit and wait. Usually in his favourite chair, sometimes in his office monitoring the dark web for illegal communication channels, searching for any clues as to when she would come for him. Of course, he would find nothing, she worked alone, but it filled his day and made him feel as if he was doing something.

Two days had passed since she had entered her nest and, daring to emerge briefly at night, Shoshanna would give her body a much needed stretch and rest. Minutes later, after reviewing the surroundings for signs of activity, she would return to her position and simply watch her target, waiting for the right routine to appear, making her task easier.

At sunrise on the third day, she was alerted by the arrival of two cars parking up very close to the assumed location of Abel Torah. Focusing her binoculars with the maximum magnification filters, she stared, transfixed, at the two cars. The detail she could see was indeed incredible.

Shoshanna's training and instinct kicked in as she mentally tallied what she saw. *Four men, two professional drivers, engines running*, she noted. *The other two are carrying semi-automatic weapons, probably also handguns, earpiece in, comms with someone.*

Lifting her head to give her eyes a moment's relief, she returned her gaze to the binoculars and carried on collating her mental inventory.

Run-flat tires, Armourlite doors and bullet-proof glass. Protected fuel tanks. The situation suddenly became a lot clearer. *Someone's getting ready to leave*, she thought to herself, biting down slightly on her lip in concentration. Was Torah going somewhere? Could this just be a coincidence or had he somehow been alerted to her presence, nearby, watching and waiting to zero in.

Shoshanna quickly ran through her options. If she were to ready her weapons and attack, would she be able to slow or even penetrate the armoured vehicles? She would have to do so under fire herself, no doubt. *No, bad idea, wait*, she thought. From the corner of her concealed vantage point, she saw further movement.

Bodyguard one, she noted. *Where's the other? It doesn't feel right*, her hackles rose as she leaned forward slightly, trying to locate the other guard.

Still further movement. Her hand tightened against the fore stock of her sniper rifle. She knew the shot was not clean, therefore, not worth taking, but instinctively, she was aware that something was going down and her hand held the gun tight.

She didn't have to wait long for the puzzle to come together. When Abel Torah's wife and two children came quickly out of the house, and were shepherded into the first car, followed by luggage being thrown by the other guard into the boot of the second vehicle, she knew that he was aware of her intentions. Torah knew she was close.

The task had just got a little harder. No hostages or bargaining chips now. No distraction of family when it happened for real. Torah knew that he was being watched and was preparing for the attack. Moving his family to safety and not following with them meant he knew this was a last stand. A last stand for them both and just what she had hoped for. There was, however, one complication. Connor Law was very likely in the area and was the one who had triggered the end game.

The two cars pulled away and down the dirt track, out of the estate and onto the tarmac road towards the town, and no doubt, the closest airport. Whilst Shoshanna knew she could easily take out the drivers and battle with the bodyguards, she decided to let them pass without incident. The wife and children would be easy pickings but it was him she was after. It would be easier for her without the innocent present, so she would only have to deal with the guilty. She watched them disappear into the distance.

Turning her attention back to the real target, she put the binoculars down and released her tight grip on the rifle. As best she could, she leaned back, allowing herself to momentarily lose sight of the buildings.

"Ok, my former friend, a clean fight it is, then. Just the four of us…" she said quietly but out loud to herself. Her expression changed and her eyes closed a little as she corrected herself, looking left towards the direction of the closest town, "And, of course, as many of them that he has brought with him."

She knew Law would not be alone, but she didn't know exactly how much backup he had. Her plan needed an element of flexibility along with the intense ruthless precision.

As the sun started to rise high, with scant warmth to release on an autumn Scottish day, she decided to wait and move out that night.

"First strike tonight, then. Let's level the playing field and then see what happens," she said to herself.

She would attack them first, before they had the chance to move in on her. Moving the family away was a clever ploy. It freed Torah and Law to go after her with no need to leave protection behind for the family.

First strike is mine, she thought as she settled back down into her sniper's nest and waited for the darkness to envelope her surroundings once again.

Chapter 18
Fight

Darkness had fallen across the estate. The moon was bright, but moving as she did, against the hill's slopes and craggy features, its light did not reveal Shoshanna's position. Indeed, the brightness of the moon is often the friend of the special forces operator. Moving at angles against the landscape is a practice that all would learn during training. It was a strategy that was well known to Connor Law, who expected her to attack tonight.

He was sure she would have seen the two cars take the family away earlier and it would trigger her plan. He was especially anxious and on alert, and he passed his concerns on to his team, Jenner and Phillips. They were to operate together while he would go after her solo.

Torah and his two bodyguards acted as if nothing had changed, however, much had done so.

The gun room had been opened and weapons were positioned discreetly amid the everyday belongings of the family home. Protective gear was worn under their clothing, and the thermal cameras were active and ready.

Without actually knowing for sure, but suspecting, Abel Torah waited for two former friends and colleagues. He knew she was out there, somewhere in the darkness, and he suspected that Connor Law was also, searching for her and watching out for him. It was a strange sensation, sitting there among what remained of his family life – little things he had taken for granted – would resume today as it had every other. The still-muddy boots of the children lined up by the kitchen porch; the splashed colour of the paintings stuck messily to the fridge door...

When she startled the fox, Shoshanna was reassured that she was moving with great stealth. The animal scampered off as if in shame that a person had got so close to it – the night-time predator, surprised by the clumsy, noisy humans.

Shoshanna knelt and waited for a few minutes. She could not risk the scrambling fox alerting someone else close by. She waited and she listened, her night-vision goggles working overtime as she surveyed her surroundings.

Nothing... she thought to herself.

Now back in control of her racing heartbeat, she saw a group of resting deer in the distance, bedding down for the night. They were right in the path of her route. She counted around twenty, aware they would prove a harder task to keep calm and not alert her presence to Connor Law.

She set off again, low and hidden away from the moonlight. Changing her course a little, so not to be fully downwind of the resting deer herd, her ears pricked up at the unmistakable sound of an approaching helicopter.

Fuck. I can't have been spotted, just can't, she thought. *Ok, so they know I'm here, but a search helicopter? No, it can't be for me.*

Thoughts and fears raced around her mind as she quickly looked for a more secure hiding place, all the time aware that the deer were very likely to react to the whirring blades of the helicopter passing close overhead. As she looked for somewhere to hide from it, she suddenly changed her mind.

Now convinced that the helicopter was not related to her movements or her presence, Shoshanna decided to use it to accelerate her passage past the deer.

"When they stir, I go, fast," she again spoke to herself, although this time a little out loud. "The heli's perfect, that's what's stirring them, not me now." She allowed herself to laugh a bit, thinking that Connor Law would surmise the same thing when he saw the chopper approaching the herd.

It worked perfectly.

As the helicopter flew past at around two hundred feet, the deer stumbled to their hooves and scampered in all directions searching for their own cover. As they did so, Shoshanna ran amongst them. She had made sure she knew exactly where the stag was and as she moved, she pushed and punched her way quickly past the few that had not seen her soon enough to veer away. Within seconds, she was through the herd and moving into

163

the trees. She was now within range of her sniper rifle from the target house.

Several minutes passed. Shoshanna moved to a new secure position amongst the trees, and again listened and searched her surroundings. Again, nothing seemed to be out of place. Breathing deeply, yet, quietly, to regain control of her heartbeat, she began to assemble her rifle from the parts wrapped individually in her rucksack.

Connor Law had seen the deer run and watched the helicopter fly past, but he had missed the stealthy figure moving through and beyond the fearful animals. He had, however, assumed that Shoshanna would have used the disturbance to make a rapid movement and change of location. After all, they trained together and it's what he would have done.

He repositioned his night-vision goggles and, allowing the moonlight to stream fully into the optics, he looked for where he would have gone, had the situation been reversed. He too saw the trees and quickly calculated the distance from there to the target – Torah.

In range, he thought to himself as he realised the situation had likely taken a turn for the worse. *For an operator as good as her, somewhere in the trees, with a serious weapon, Torah will be in range. She has to be there, just has to be.* He finished looking around and past the trees, his gaze returning to the wooded area. The hairs stood to attention on his neck. He swallowed hard and had to move his body to allow it to happen more easily.

Something inside him was telling him *he* was also in range. He too was close to his target, and he still didn't know what would happen if and when he saw her again.

"John, please take a look round the perimeter, will you? I just feel uneasy tonight," said Torah, sitting at the kitchen table and trying carefully to avoid any position directly exposed to a window.

"Sir, yes, straight away," came the reply from his first bodyguard as he stood and upholstered his handgun before walking out into the cold of the night.

When the bullet left the barrel, John Sanderson had less than half a second to live. The 7.62 round smashed into his skull at a velocity of over eight hundred metres per second, and John

Sanderson's head lifted off and away from his shoulders. The headless torso fell heavy to the ground but out of earshot of the others inside the Torah family home.

She had waited several seconds until he had passed far enough away from the main building and closer towards the perimeter vegetation. The night would conceal his body for a while until the curious foxes became braver as their stomachs grew emptier.

Shoshanna knew it was a clean kill and that she had not compromised her position. The suppressor had kept the flash and noise down to a minimum, so she was comfortable to sit tight and wait.

That was easy, she thought to herself. *One more and whoever Law's brought, then it's just me and him.*

However, her confidence was short-lived. A few minutes passed and with each moment, she started to feel more uneasy. She knew that very soon the occupants of the house would start to wonder what was keeping the bodyguard; but something else was bothering her. The first kill had been easy. Perhaps, too easy.

The bodyguards have never come out to check the perimeter this early before. Why now, why tonight? Her eyes darted back and forth as she tried to figure out what was arousing her suspicions. *Why would he do something tonight that he has not done before?*

She moved a little uneasily now and suddenly felt as if she was being watched.

It's fine. Shoshanna tried to reassure herself that tonight's broken routine, on the very night she was going in after Abel Torah, was mere coincidence.

Fuck, she said to herself as she rapidly packed her gear and started to move out, knowing that her trained instincts needed heeding.

For over ten years, across the world's war zones, her gut feeling had kept her alive. Now it was telling her something wasn't right and now was not the moment to ignore it.

Shoshanna had learned a long time ago that when the senses pushed themselves into her head and forced their will on the decision-making process, the body must obey and do so quickly.

Now away from her first killing point, and moving rapidly across and partly down the slope, she challenged her eyes and ears to see, and hear everything. Her breathing remained calm and quiet but her thoughts were a thousand a second.

Threat, exposure, being seen, being shot at, her mind managed the manic and rushed thinking well.

She had not seen the birds fly out and away from the tree as she passed at speed beneath them. But he had. Connor saw the movement above the branches and wondered if it was her. He could not be sure. It could have been anything, but it could also have been her.

With no way of knowing for sure, he continued to move slowly and steadily towards the wooded area he suspected she was in, or, perhaps, had been concealed within.

Moments later, with Law on the edge of the trees, looking in and listening, and his prey a short way off, crouching, hidden and waiting, a strange silence and stillness returned to the hillside. Even the creatures of the night appeared to be waiting for something to happen next.

Shoshanna looked skyward and saw nothing but what she believed was an owl looking down upon her. It hooted as it glided away, seemingly fearful of her ruthless precision, choosing not to seek out its own target to kill and feed on at the moment.

Keep watching over me, my feathered friend, she thought to herself as she took her stare away from the fleeing owl and back into the glass of the night-vision apparatus.

Operationally a world apart, the two enemies played their uncertain cat and mouse game. Neither knew that they crouched and waited less than two hundred metres from each other.

Law took his secure phone out and rang a pre-designated number. It rang once on the recipient's device and he ended the call. No noise left his own phone. The silence of the moment was deafening.

Diane Philips rose to her feet and the movement brought her colleague Jenner to action.

Both picked up their rucksacks and left the building.

In moments, the jeep was on the move along the dirt track, and towards the estate and the home of Torah. Their approach would not be discreet nor would it be disguised. Instead, Law's

Section 2 colleagues would park abruptly and sharply, the jeep's tires throwing dust into the night sky.

Shoshanna heard them coming before she saw them. She knew that they would know she was close and she knew by the overtness of their approach, these people, probably with Connor Law, did not care that they would be seen and heard. This tactic confused her slightly.

They had been instructed to make a bold entrance. Perhaps, a show of strength, Diane had initially thought, as she hopped out of the parked vehicle. But any notion of strength was quickly dispelled when the driver, exiting the jeep, collapsed in mortal agony, the victim of a seven-inch serrated knife forced through his neck and out the other side. Unable to cry out, he was dead before he fell to the ground. The only noise was his dead-weight body thumping down hard onto the side of the jeep and alerting the two men inside the property.

The speed and the ferocity of the attack had caught Diane Philips off guard.

She had her gun in hand, yet, as it began its movement upwards towards the central mass of the female assassin who'd appeared behind the driver's falling body, eyes filled with fire and fury, her final vision was the glint of metal against the moonlight, then nothing. She fell as heavy and as hard as the bullet that had entered, and then exited her skull, now a thousand feet away, seeking a second target in the night.

Shoshanna emptied a second bullet into Diane's chest, but not before bending briefly to retrieve her knife from the neck of her first victim, the blade coming away easily out and through the flesh of Jenner's vocal chords.

Four remained.

Those four knew for sure that only they remained.

Law knew his two colleagues lay dead at the hands of his former lover – he had risked sending them into the target area loud and clear. Torah and the man who had been his bodyguard for fifteen long years sat inside the house, and waited. And Shoshanna stood in the shadow of the building, adrenalin fuelled, with a heart as black as the night sky.

All four knew that the endgame approached at speed. Law now abandoned any notion of stealth and stood up. Dropping his rucksack and rifle, he ran towards the main building with his handgun only.

If he truly knew her and his former boss inside the building, he would be allowed the approach and entrance into the killing zone. She would wait and watch; her heart, no doubt, beating at double speed because of her current situation and the imminent arrival of Connor Law.

Inside, the two men sat in silence. Both armed and both expecting violence. For one, it would come all too soon.

Then, when Law slowed his pace and walked near the jeep, he raised both hands into the air. While he could not see her, he knew she was watching him.

He stood for a moment at the body of his former colleague in Section 2 and then glanced over towards the other. Emotionless, he walked on and towards the main door.

"Torah, it's Law and I'm coming in," he said as his hand clasped the doorknob.

Inside, Torah raised a hand to his one remaining bodyguard to instruct him not to react and to indicate that this person was indeed allowed to come in unchallenged.

As the door opened, the light from inside momentarily caught Law's face, his jaw set with determination, as he turned to the darkness and spoke.

Shoshanna held her breath as she saw him. The face she once loved and the man she would have left the service for in an instant. She was hidden in the shadows only yards away, yet, he could not see her. He could, however, feel her presence and thought he could hear her breathing.

Then he spoke, the first words directed at her in a long time. His voice was haunting yet strangely warming.

"Sho, come in when you're ready. We're waiting. Don't be too long, it's cold out here." And with his voice echoing in her ears and her mind, the chink of light disappeared and darkness returned as he entered the building, and closed the door behind him.

Connor had figured it out. He knew she would not kill him on the spot, but instead, would accept his invite to enter the building, and face both him and Torah – her target. Her founder. The man who had set her on the path to what she had become today. Torah had started it for her, and both men knew she would want to understand what evil hid in her mind and the darkness of her soul.

Connor Law felt that he might have figured it out the day before. Figured out why this renegade soldier had turned. The school incident, the desert kill and the others... He knew that answers were coming, but he also knew he held a small flame deep down inside him for the one true love that he had promised a carefree life to. But he betrayed her that day when he stepped onto the helicopter and back into active service.

He knew there were answers coming, but he also knew there was likely pain and denial. He was ready for what was going to happen next.

Law entered the room and nodded to his former commander, indicating that Shoshanna, the person who wanted to kill him, was coming.

Before Law took a seat, Torah turned to his one remaining long-term bodyguard and family friend, and apologised.

"I will make sure they are looked after, my friend." Abel Torah shot him point-blank in the chest, his friend's face twisted in sudden horror at the betrayal. His bodyguard fell to the ground, taking the chair he was sitting on with him.

Law stood and watched as Torah walked over to the dead man, and, gently closing his eyelids, repeated his words, "I swear I will look after your family, my loving friend." And standing back up, he signalled Law to sit. Law pulled a chair up at the table, and both men did indeed sit and wait.

Now there were three.

Having heard the noise of the gunshot, Shoshanna made the assumption that it was now just them. Just her former lover and her former commander. She was correct.

For several minutes, all three waited and again, a strange silence descended. Again, the night animals seemed frozen, as if time stood still. *What was to happen next?* They must have thought.

Then, raising her handgun to chest height, Shoshanna gripped the door handle and turned it.

Chapter 19
Reveal

The two men sat in silence, their handguns in reach and deliberately visible to anyone who would care to look. They knew she would come.

Connor Law was the more uncomfortable of the two. He wondered how he would feel when he saw her again. He would have killed her on the private beach in Angola but had hoped then to do it at a distance. Whatever was to happen in the next few minutes would be face to face.

Law sat and watched the doorway. The hairs on his neck stood up despite the sweat running down from his head, under his shirt and down his back. The emotion was strong, even for a trained soldier and killer. He was, after all, still human.

Abel Torah sat at an angle to the door. He almost had his back to it but could see it partly from the reflection in the window. He knew how she would enter. He knew she needed to control the room and have the initiative. He knew he had a difficult conversation coming with his favoured assassin and he was prepared to give her the lead she would need.

Both men sat and waited in silence.

The irony of the wait was not missed on either man but they didn't speak of it. They sat and waited for a lethal killer to enter the room, hell bent on killing them, and they chose not to ready themselves or even defend their position. Such was their belief that she would not discharge her weapon when she entered but would, in that moment, decide to manage the situation instead.

Shoshanna walked the hallway, still expecting a firefight but also a little confused about the gunfire she heard and Law's words to her. She had dispelled thoughts of a trap, but her training would not allow her to announce her arrival. So, she walked the hall a careful and slow inch at a time.

The ninety seconds it took her to reach the kitchen door, the only possible location of her two foes having searched earlier rooms. Time seemed to stop as she moved through the house. Torah sat and closed his eyes. He could have waited for hours but both Shoshanna and Connor Law needed something, anything, to happen quickly. Their blood beat fast and furious, and no amount of controlled breathing could limit the pounding of heart on chest.

When Law saw the slight shadow under the door change shape, he knew she was directly outside and he wanted to instinctively reach for his gun but physically restrained himself. She too would now know that her position had been compromised and she also had to restrain herself from acting accordingly.

Every sinew of her body was screaming at her to rush the room. They were her targets. They were her end game and her absolution. But she chose not to. On this occasion, Shoshanna simply pushed the door open.

The light from the kitchen flooded the hallway, her careful and stealthy walk along the corridor now totally wasted due to her chosen method of entry.

She saw Torah first, his undeniably small but stocky frame shortened by the pressure of parachute jump after jump leaving his spine compressed and twisted. She felt the jolt of familiarity as she glanced at his profile. With less hair than she remembered, her eyes took in the features that she once admired and the face she once followed with absolute loyalty. With his firm, high cheek bones and slightly protruding chin line, he still had a powerful and commanding presence.

She saw the handgun on the table next to him and tightened her hold on her own weapon, raised and ready for use.

Then she saw him. He had watched her enter and had again found it hard not to grab his own weapon. He looked tired, she thought, trying hard not to let the emotion of seeing him again show on her face. It had been so long, too long. Her breath caught as he looked her directly in the eye and their gaze locked for a fleeting, intense second.

The moment was over in a heartbeat, although it felt much longer to the three once-trusted ex-colleagues… ex-friends. They were back together for the first time in years. But there was no celebration, no handshake – certainly no drinks in the barracks mess room to follow. This time, she had the lead and she instantly knew she had been given it.

Shoshanna took her eyes off her former lover, her first real love and struggled hard in her conscience to hate him. He had betrayed her love. He had chosen service and country over her. She tried and failed to hate him, but she did choose not to look directly at him anymore.

"Shoshanna, welcome," Abel Torah started. It was as if she had never left his side or his service.

"Please, my friend, take a seat, sit with us, we mean you no further harm," he continued. Turning to face her and lifting himself off his chair, Torah moved a little closer to her and gestured towards a seat near the table. A position that he knew would give her continued leverage and mastery of the room. Shoshanna looked at the offered chair; she also knew that she could sit where directed and still have the upper hand.

"Sit, please," and with that, Torah moved his own chair further around, now facing her proposed seat. He then sat back down. His own weapon now positioned further out of reach.

"I sit when and where I choose," she growled back at him, all the time keeping the most dangerous of her two marks within her peripheral vision. Shoshanna had yet to see where Law's weapon was and she remained unsettled because of it.

"Gun and hands, you…" she said, glancing at Law.

He duly obliged and pushed the handgun into sight across a small side table next to where he sat.

"Hands – up now," she ordered, raising her weapon towards him. Connor obligingly stood and removed his jacket, slowly and deliberately, allowing her to see he had no secondary concealed weapon.

"Down there," she said, pointing back to his chair. "And keep your hands visible." With the command fulfilled, she kicked the side table over and his gun skittled a short distance away across the stone floor, far enough that she could land three clean shots into him should he reach for it.

"Why don't I kill you both right here, right now?" she said, eyeing the two men curiously, starting to feel more in control of the situation. She remained confused as to why she had been invited in and not attacked as she stalked her target. However, like the two men in front of her, she had a perverse desire to see this through to the end. It was time for the ultimate showdown and if that meant all cards being laid bare, so be it. The tension in the room was palpable.

"Why don't you kill us, Shoshanna?" Torah asked, his voice commanding despite the vulnerable situation he was in… they were all in. "Why don't you pull the trigger, and end the turmoil and pain once and for all? We sit and wait for you, Shoshanna. We sit here and both wait for you, my best and my favourite, to end the killing, here, in this place. We're here, Shoshanna, and we need to know what's going on." Torah settled further back into his seat and waited for her response.

Feeling challenged, Shoshanna raised her gun once again and aimed it straight at Torah's head. She knew she would not pull the trigger. He knew this also but sat still, allowing her the easy target.

She moved closer to him and, stepping over the body of his former guard, Shoshanna signalled to Connor to move towards Torah.

"So, what did he do wrong, Abel?" she asked, glancing momentarily down at the dead man now lying behind her.

"He remained alive in advance of you being here, my dear," said Torah. "It needed to be us, just us; it was always going to be just us." With this, Torah stood defiantly and walked over to a desk against the far wall. Law had moved closer to Torah, so Shoshanna remained in control of the situation – she felt comfortable enough to let her former commander move against her wishes.

He pulled out a deep drawer and reached in. Out came a blue bottle. She recognised it instantly. Connor Law smiled.

"I am told that the one on the beach was finished, Shoshanna, so I could not allow you to come to my humble home without offering you a drink," he said with a calming smile across his face.

Law sat on the edge of the window. She allowed this; he had not moved towards the gun on the floor and he seemed not to have a second weapon. She could be wrong but she let it go this time.

"Johnny Walker Private Label, chief," he said. "Like the one I saw on that Angolan beach recently, opened and emptied without me," Law went on, slightly mocking Shoshanna.

She stared at him, her face betraying both sadness and confusion.

Torah brought the bottle to the main table and returned to the drawer, emerging with three shot glasses. He poured three full measures and handed two out to his unexpected guests.

Law downed his drink instantly, while Torah offered his glass up to her to toast.

The angry frown on her face told him there would be no chink of glasses, so he took a drink and sat back down in his seat.

"Shoshanna, sit, please," he said as his hand extended towards her chair. She looked over, assessing her options. The position still allowed her control over the whole room, and with no further surprises likely to come from behind her, she did as suggested and sat down.

With a gun in one hand and a whisky in the other, the confusion was beginning to grow inside her.

"So, Law… why…" she began, but was interrupted.

"Sho, you know my name. Come on," said Law, looking her directly in the eye.

Shoshanna looked away from him towards Torah. "I call you whatever the fuck I want, Law. I am the one holding," she sneered in reply as she moved the gun a tiny amount to reinforce her comment.

Connor Law smiled. "As you wish, Agnon."

She took control again. "So, Law, why did you invite me in? And tell me why I spared your life when you did so," she said, happier now she got to finish her sentence and get the words out she desperately to.

"Agnon, I did not invite you in. You invited yourself when the memories started to come back. They have started again, haven't they?" he said, knowing the answer and turning to look at Torah. Turning back to her, he continued, "I was just the facilitator, the messenger. And the other point to remember: no one shoots the messenger." She saw a tiny smirk appear on his lips. There they were, the three of them. Three assassins, with love lost between them and an explosive situation waiting to happen, yet, Connor Law smirked at the funny quip he had just made to his former lover and soulmate.

Shoshanna was slightly unnerved by his confidence and the ease with which Torah seemed to manipulate her to sit. He was no longer her commander, but she seemed to instinctively do as she was instructed.

She suddenly knew what she had dreaded about seeing them again. A killer she was, but with her former commander Torah and with the tiniest of love left in her heart, she knew that she would never be in control. Shoshanna looked at the two men. They looked back but said nothing. Both men appeared to know already what she was beginning to wake up to.

Then the mood suddenly changed. A dark air swept across the room.

When he spoke, she likened the pressure change to the opening of a parachute. Her heart missed a beat. Every muscle and sinew in her body seemed to stop, and go into shock, waiting for the next big thump.

When the thump did come, it was not physical like exiting a plane and releasing a parachute. Instead, the thump was the strongest of emotional hammer blows she had ever experienced.

"Shoshanna, you need to know, don't you? You are likely having sleepless nights and, I would suggest, battles in your head?" Then, as Torah rose off his chair, she slumped like lead further into hers.

She clasped her handgun tighter. She knew it was a last act of defiance but at the same time, she knew it was a battle she would lose this time around.

Her heart tried to burst out of her chest as Abel Torah walked over to her and sat, placing a hand on her knee.

Her gun hand would not lift. She looked down her arm at the weapon, but it did not do as she felt it should. Instead, she let him in unchallenged.

From the corner of her left eye, she saw Connor Law rise up off the window ledge. He moved fully into view, but no closer, allowing his former commander to do as he thought best.

"Tell me about the new battles, my dear. Tell me what you see in your mind when you close your eyes and try to sleep." Although Torah seemed to stop and wait for a reply, he had not finished yet.

"Philadelphia… we know you were in Philadelphia at the time David Spencer was assassinated. Killed with a rare poison only used by a select few. Us, we are the select few. Do you see Spencer when you close your eyes? Do you still blame him, you know, for the blue on blue killing of members of your troop?"

Shoshanna kept her face as unemotional as possible. She did not want to even consider that they may have been tracking her, watching her, or worse, letting her kill at will over the last few months. Her head buzzed with confusion. *Do they really know or are they grabbing and hoping for a reaction*, she thought. *Strong, stay strong.*

Torah kept going. He kept pushing her with his words and as he did so, the fight started to leave her. For the first time she could ever remember, she had nothing left to attack with. Her hand released the gun. Both men saw it. Both men knew the fight had left her. Torah kept the verbal challenge going.

"The Nevada job was pure brilliance, Shoshanna. To get Mike Ridge on his patch, at his game, was brilliant. I particularly liked that one. It made me smile." Torah turned to Law. "Water, please, my friend." And Law went to the sink to pour a glass for them both. "You know, they found the other body a week or so later. The cameraman. He had set off in the complete wrong direction from the closest town. I wonder why?" he said as he smiled again. "Well, when I say 'found', his face and arms were gnawed off by coyotes or something, but his dental records identified him. I guess you blamed Ridge for the scrap in Mogadishu? The one when you arrived to the fight too early and unscheduled?"

Torah's onslaught was relentless, only slowing to allow him to drink some water.

Suddenly, Law spoke up, "Damn good fight with the big Russian. I don't think I could have done much better."

"You were…" but she was interrupted.

"No, I wasn't, but Bohdan was and I believe he pocketed a few dollars before finding himself garrotted in his bed one night. Shame, that."

Torah stood and walked to the window, looking out into the darkness of the night sky.

Shoshanna sat and stared at him, reflecting on what Law had said about Vitschencko and Bohdan. Had she been betrayed?

Was I set up? she thought as she contemplated her next move. But, before she could find the words to speak, Torah broke the temporary silence.

"Who threw the incendiary grenade into the school that day, Shoshanna? Who was hell bent on killing anyone who dared to threaten your family and those under your command?"

Her head reeled with the emotional hammer blow.

"No, no…" she stammered. "It was that mad fuck, Vitschencko. You are wrong! You were not there; you are wrong, it was him!" she spat through gritted teeth, not daring to believe that it could actually have been any other way.

"Ok, Shoshanna, you need to believe that. I get it. The pain in your heart must be really bad. That school… the burning children…" Torah returned from the window and stood over her. Shoshanna, more submissive and threatened by the prospect of further horror exposed in her subconscious, accepted him dominating her, like a puppy submits to stronger pack leader to avoid further conflict.

She could almost feel his breath on her neck as he leaned down a little to whisper quietly in her ear.

"Helene Marte was not responsible for the op going south that day, was she? And Kyle Scott at the British Foreign Office, could he even have known that the heli had malfunctioned, that the enemy were greater in number and waiting? Do you know he fought for weeks to get a team in to rescue you, but they wouldn't let him? Now his wife and young son have no father. A father you killed to satisfy your own mistaken beliefs." Shoshanna breathed in sharply and tried to focus. Instantly, he changed back to the Abel Torah she needed at that moment.

"My dear Shoshanna, my best, my very best. I love you like you were my own daughter. Who do you think watched over you when Marte's team was destroyed in a freak ambush for which she was not to blame? Who got them back? We were in support and in the shadows. We are always in the shadows. Every time you went off comms on a live operation, I made sure you had support ready and able to get involved."

Shoshanna's eyes filled with tears, reluctant tears, for she could not remember when she had last cried. Even when she heard of her mother's untimely death, she did not spill a tear but instead, felt her heart blacken a little more.

177

Torah looked over to Law, then gestured towards the door. It was time for him to leave and take a walk.

She did not see the subtle instruction but she did see Law stand up and walk out. Before the door had fully closed behind him, Connor Law heard Torah address the broken figure sitting in the dimness of the room, wide-eyed and staring at her hands. "Just us, my lovely, now just us," and he knew exactly what that meant.

Law stepped out into the darkness and the chill of the Highlands' night, each breath visible as he walked further away from the building.

Fine, right, it's Torah. It's the right thing to do, he told himself as he walked farther away down the track. *She's a liability, she's loose.* But his thoughts meant nothing to him. He did not truly believe them.

Connor Law's heart thumped in his chest; his mind panicked as his thoughts raced. He saw her. His mind forced her back in front of him. He saw them, together, on that private beach in the sun, laughing and happy. The only time when he didn't think of the blood and the death. Now Torah was about to kill the memories. She was in a house with him, and her life was about to end and Connor Law knew it. He was letting this happen.

Law stood and faced the hills, as if searching for an answer, but he saw nothing. With darkness came anonymity. His whole life had been darkness – the killing and the death. His darkest moments were when he'd let killings happen that didn't need to. "Greater good, they need to die, people need to die, even her," he said quietly but out loud.

Inside, Torah held Shoshanna firm in a warm and loving embrace as she sat. With one hand he clasped her strongest arm, her gun hand. He spoke to himself just out loud. He said a soothing, gentle prayer into her ear.

Shoshanna felt warm. She again felt loved and for a few moments, she felt happy. She knew what was coming. She had prepared for this moment for weeks. She had stepped into the house knowing she would never leave it. She was ready.

She had just been told that everything she had thought, everything she believed to be true, was not so. That she was actually the perpetrator of evil violence against the wrongly targeted or wrongly accused. She knew the punishment was coming soon for her sins.

For a second, a million flashbacks filled her head. She could hardly breathe. Could he be right? Could Torah be right and it was her all along, all the time? She panicked but she kept the fear inside.

Connor Law turned back to look at the house. He knew what was going to happen. He knew he would never see her again, alive, unless…

Torah calmly reached into his jacket to the gun holster fixed across his chest. Unbuttoning the leather strap, he pulled the gun out and into sight. She could feel his movement and suspected he was positioning himself for the kill. She hoped it would be quick.

She didn't look up, nor did her heartbeat rise. She was accepting her fate. She deserved this end and she waited peacefully for it.

He finished the quiet prayer and moved the gun towards her head. She had allowed him a clean shot without risk to himself. He knew she would not resist.

When Shoshanna felt the cold, hard tip of the barrel push against her head, she instantly heard the unmistakable sound of gunfire. In one confused millisecond, Shoshanna believed that she was dead. That she was somewhere else, hell, perhaps, but no longer in the mortal world.

When she felt Torah fall across her lap and the hold on her right arm was released, she opened her eyes.

What she saw was confusing in that initial moment of death, which she presumed she was experiencing. Standing outside a now shattered glass window, holding a gun out in front, was Connor Law – her former lover and the only person who once ever truly understood her.

For one unbalanced moment, she wondered if she might be in hell. It was all she could dare to think, before a very different reality slowly started to dawn upon her.

Shoshanna stared at the broken glass, and as he lowered his arm and moved away from the window towards the door, she kept her glance outward. She now knew Torah was dead, and that the warm liquid running out onto boots and trousers was his blood. She didn't yet know why, however. Again, Shoshanna waited for something to happen. Tearful and emotionally weak, she sat motionless.

The door eventually opened and Law walked in. It seemed to have been an age since the shot and now he returned back into her life for the third time. This time, he was there to save her, to extend her life, but she did not know why.

He walked over towards her, and grabbed the slumped body of his former friend and commander, pushing it off her, watching as it fell down to the floor.

"Shoshanna, it wasn't meant to be this way. I couldn't talk him out of it. Believe me, I tried, but he needed you dead. You were becoming too great a liability. When it went public, his reputation and that of the unit back in Israel would be shot. Our allies would not trust us and we would have to operate against emerging threats alone," said Law, struggling to remain professional and keep the emotion out of his voice. He visibly softened as he stepped towards her.

"That day in Angola, at the beach, I didn't come to kill you. I came to warn you. But you had gone, vanished minutes before I got there. And now he's dead too – he didn't need to be. If I had just managed to get to you, I could have persuaded you to disappear, to stop the killing, perhaps, even to explain it, so the nightmares would leave you and you could have a life back again, but…" He was interrupted by Shoshanna, finally back in the present.

"I knew it was you. My heart told me it was you coming after me. I came here voluntarily. I was ready for death; I remain ready for it. I have nothing to live for." She paused, trying to catch the emotion in her voice. "Once, long ago, in happier days, which I can still remember, you were my Connor Law." Shoshanna stood up and walked to the table, where a glass of water still stood.

She sipped on the water, and turned back to face him and spoke in a warm and loving tone.

"Why did you do it? Why did I not die tonight?"

She was convinced, as she looked into his eyes, she saw the glint that comes only from the start of tears. Allowing him the dignity of an answer without the pressure of her direct stare, she turned to the glass of water and placed both hands on the table.

She would never receive an answer. There would be no further conversation that night in a hunter's home, in the cold and dark hills north of a Scottish town.

He walked right up to her and with his breath on her neck he placed his palm down on the table in front of her, leaving something next to the glass. He then abruptly turned and walked out the house.

She knew he was leaving her. She knew that he felt the same as Torah had felt. She was a liability; she could not be trusted, and she was a danger to his unit, his brothers and his country.

She allowed her eyes to fill with tears, for she had hoped he would come back into her life. But he had again chosen service over human love. She knew he would soon be back in Israel and on operation, and she knew that she would always wonder what could have happened and if they would ever meet again.

Shoshanna looked at the table in front of her where Connor had seconds previously laid his hand. On it was a neatly folded piece of paper. She did not want to touch it – she could see the word 'Judas' burnt onto it in her mind's eye. She felt like she had betrayed him and her unit. She was Judas. This piece of paper was most likely the reason why he left her once more. Why he never properly loved her, or why she was not worthy of his love again. This was the final nail in her metaphorical coffin, the end of her emotional journey.

She sat there for some time, figuring perhaps an hour had passed since he had left the kitchen and her life for good, before she looked back at that folded piece of paper. She could smell the growing stench of Torah's congealing blood on the floor and sense his body hardening as the fluids seeped into the wooden boards.

She reached for the paper and crumpled it in her hand. She wanted it to burn her; she wanted it to disappear like some magic trick when she opened her fingers but neither happened. Instead, her strength slowly returned and with it, her curiosity grew.

She released her grip on the paper and started to unfold it.

She stared at the words written there.

It was not a rationale for his love of service over her. It was a simple few words and fewer numbers.

It simply read 'Flat B, Richardson Avenue, Pimlico, London, 07779 009132'.

It was not signed by Connor but she recognised his handwriting. She read his final note, 'She's waiting for you. She loves you as I did once. Go to her and be happy.'

When the realisation struck, Shoshanna clutched her throat in surprise.

With the piece of paper gripped in her hand, she allowed herself to exhale. Slumping back down onto the chair, she stared at the neat writing again. She allowed herself to smile. *They had been watching 'me' as well*, she thought. They watched everyone and yet, he had not intercepted her at any time. Her mind was working away in overtime, trying to clear the confusion and focus simply on the joy, and the new opportunity.

Chapter 20
Hello

She couldn't stay in the house that night. It stank of two dead bodies – the bodyguard and her former father figure, Abel Torah. That said, she was scared to leave. The one man who had ever truly understood her, Law, had left her alone with the dead men and disappeared into the trees.

Was he still there, waiting? Was he watching?

She found it hard to bring herself to leave the house, but when she did so, she left unexpectedly stronger than when she had entered it. A new life had sprung up inside her. She was Shoshanna Agnon, but she was no longer the same woman who killed and killed again with ease.

She walked out of the house leaving the door open, the lights from the hallway illuminating the front of the building. Soon enough, the authorities would find the carnage, and try and fail to retrace the steps of those involved. The local police would then call in the experts but by then, it would be too late. It was always too late when her former Unit was involved.

Shoshanna cut a lonely figure, walking down the stone path and out of the estate. She did not look into the woods now, accepting he had left her life for good.

It was raining in London. It always seemed to rain when Shoshanna was in London. This day, like the past two, was rainy and windy.

This day, like the previous two, she had watched Lisa shepherd her two young children into and out of school. Out of the car, under the umbrella and the reverse several hours earlier. Between the school runs, Shoshanna watched her, wondering if she had the right. She questioned whether she should interfere with a family's life in order to finally better her own.

On this day, the third day of watching, she knew the answer.

The children were sent packing into school and Lisa walked back across the wet playground, dancing around the puddles. She looked down at the ground mostly, so as not to get her shoes wet.

She had almost reached the gate out to the street when her eyes saw two neatly tied, black laced-up boots in her way. She stopped her puddle dancing and slowly looked upwards. The blood in her veins pulsed faster as her heart began to pound, recognising the person in front of her.

Shoshanna struggled for words. She managed only one. "Hello."

"Hello."

The two women simply stared at each other. A few seconds passed before they were interrupted by a parent.

"Watch, love, you're in the way of the gate," said the other mother jovially. The two friends moved aside. Still no words were made between them.

Lisa eventually broke the awkward silence. "How are you, Sho? Where've you been?" Lisa's words were hesitatingly spoken. Even she knew that the unannounced visit was not right, that her friend had clearly followed her to her children's school and, more so, that Shoshanna was there for a purpose.

Shoshanna thought momentarily of answering her question with honesty – *I'm a trained assassin: I've killed more people than you've had hot dinners and I could break your neck in seconds with one hand* – but she bit down hard on her lip as she fought the urge to laugh at the ridiculousness of it all. Would Lisa even believe her?

Lisa stared at her unflinchingly, but still a bit anxious about the unannounced arrival of her rather strange friend. "I mean, how are you and why are you here, Sho?" she said, indicating slightly to the school playground behind her.

"Let's walk," said Shoshanna, gripping Lisa's arm with as much casualness as she could muster. With that, the two women left the confines of the school gates and walked up the street in the opposite direction of the parked family car.

"Why do I feel this to be an ultimatum, Shoshanna?" questioned Lisa.

"No ultimatum, no. A risk, my risk – my risk, not yours," Shoshanna responded, echoing Lisa's own anxiety. "I have to tell you something and you're not going to like it, Lisa. In fact,

you're going to hate what I have to say and so... my risk."
Walking a little bit closer, she lowered her voice before she
spoke again, "Ultimatum – mine, not yours."

Lisa could not yet understand what her friend meant, but she
would soon enough.

"Ultimatum: accept me and what I have done, or sentence
me to death in perpetuity."

Lisa was confused by the obscure remark and worried, not
for the first time, about the mental state of her friend. "Not here,
not yet, Sho," Lisa said as she grabbed Shoshanna's hand in a
safe and secure gesture.

"You can't have done what I have done. With two young
active kids – the cleaning involved, the crap, really the 'crap' and
stuff... no, you can't have done what I have done, my lovely."
With the next breath, Lisa pointed to the coffee shop across the
road, "After all, you're just some travel bum that lives life to the
full. Nothing too exciting, right?"

"No, you're right, Lisa: life, not my thing really, more
death..."

Lisa looked at her troubled lover and grabbed her shoulder,
steering her across the road towards the coffee shop. "Right,
double espresso for you then; let's talk."

By the time the two friends were walking the beach in the
sun, hand in hand and occasionally swimming in the waves,
laughing and lying in the heat together, most of what needed to
be said had been said.

The children were safe at home, dropped off and picked up
from school by their grandmother, desperate for her daughter to
find love and companionship again, whoever it was with. While
she had never met Shoshanna, she had heard wonderful tales of
her travel exploits.

Now, the two women were on the beach, hand in hand, on
their own secluded area of coastline that Lisa had never
considered a tourist destination.

They enjoyed the quiet sands, with a run-down hut for
accommodation and a large bag of supplies. As they entered the
shallow water, the tiny fish would come and flit around them.

"No private training this time, my little friends," said
Shoshanna, which puzzled Lisa, her face screwing up slightly.

"This time?" she quizzed.

"Nothing, Lisa, just speaking to the fish…"

They would walk the beach for a while longer and finally settle down to eat on the sand near the hut. Shoshanna started a fire and speared the fish they had caught, placing them as a spit across the flames.

"Done that before, Sho?"

"Nope, lucky first time," came the reply without lifting her gaze from the task at hand.

"Right, of course," laughed Lisa.

The flames sparked up around them as the oil from the fish started to drip down onto the fire.

The sun had an hour's life left before conceding to the moon and the stars, but the two women didn't notice it descending into the water, nor did they care.

Instead, they laughed and talked. Sometimes, Shoshanna would freeze and tell her friend a truth, but within seconds, Lisa would be back lightening the mood.

"Shoshanna, my love, did you really think I believed that you were a traveller trying to write a book?"

Shoshanna froze again.

"Sho, no one has those tattoos, sleeps with a handgun under her pillow and is a true travel rep," and with that confession, Lisa stood and walked towards the second bottle of malt whisky, in the rucksack inside the shack.

Shoshanna's handgun was also in the rucksack, but she felt an instant acceptance in her lover's last words that stopped her from hiding anymore.

"Make sure you choose the bottle over the piece," she said to Lisa.

"I know how to drink, Sho; you may need to teach me how to shoot," and simultaneously they both laughed.

Over the next few days, Shoshanna would sometimes suspect she could feel the stare of eyes on her neck but, turning rapidly towards the thick vegetation running alongside the beach, would find nothing or no one. Maybe Connor Law really had left her life for good.